Café Spice Namaste

Café Spice
Namaste

New-wave Indian cooking
with over 100 recipes

Cyrus Todiwala

EBURY PRESS
LONDON

Acknowledgements

I would like firstly to thank my wife Pervin for her unfaltering support and her faith in all that I do. Also for being so patient while I worked on this book and trying to sleep under the glare of the computer screen while I punched away at the keys until the wee hours of the morning.

A big thank you goes to my parents, who have given me all the help that I ever needed, from spending hours by my bedside when I was an asthmatic child, to enduring sleepless nights during my early baking days and supporting me in my choice of career despite their disappointment in it. I hope that I have done them proud; they are the greatest parents one could wish for.

Thanks also to Tony Hewitt, our good and dear friend, who tried out all the recipes in this book and helped me adjust them where necessary to make them suitable for use in the home. Not forgetting my team of chefs, who had to take on an additional burden while I wrote this book, particularly my wonderful head chefs Angelo and Mathias.

Lastly thanks to all the members of our team, old and new, at Café Spice Namaste, and to my business partners Michael and Martin, who have helped me to make Café Spice all that it is today.

Thank you all.

NOTE ON THE RECIPES
Unless otherwise stated, all recipes serve 4, and oil is sunflower oil.

First published in 1998

1 3 5 7 9 10 8 6 4 2

Text © 1998 Cyrus Todiwala
Photographs © Ebury Press 1998

The author has asserted his right to be identified as the author of this work under the Copyright, Designs and Patents Act 1988.

All rights reserved. No part of this publication may be reproduced, stored in a retrieval system, or transmitted in any form or by any means, electronic, mechanical, photocopying or otherwise without the prior permission of the copyright owners.

First published in the United Kingdom in 1998 by Ebury Press Random House, 20 Vauxhall Bridge Road, London SW1V 2SA

Random House Australia (Pty) Limited
20 Alfred Street, Milsons Point, Sydney,
New South Wales 2061, Australia

Random House New Zealand Limited
18 Poland Road, Glenfield, Auckland 10, New Zealand

Random House South Africa (Pty) Limited
Endulini, 5a Jubilee Road, Parktown 2193, South Africa

Random House UK Limited Reg. No. 954009

Papers used by Ebury Press are natural, recyclable products made from wood grown in sustainable forests.

A CIP catalogue record for this book is available from the British Library.

ISBN 0 09 186503 4

Edited by Jane Middleton
Photography by Philip Webb
Styling by Roísín Nield
Home economy by Sunil Vijayakar
Illustrations by Rosemary Woods

Printed and bound in Singapore by Tien Wah Press

The Café Spice Namaste restaurants are at
16 Prescot Street, London E18A2
Tel: 0171 488 9242
and
247-249 Lavender Hill, Battersea, London SW11 1JW
Tel: 0171 738 1717

Contents

Introduction

I often think of my first adventures in cooking, when I was just eight or nine years old and living in Bombay. I used to pinch Mum's *chapatis*, caramelize them in sugar or butter until crisp and then sell them for 5 *paisa* each to my cousins and sister. Mum's *chapatis*, her butter, her sugar, her gas and my profits.

When I was 12 I attempted to make my first custard by adding custard powder to boiling milk. I wanted to give my mother a surprise when she came home but even she couldn't remedy the disastrous mess that ensued. Some of my greatest learning experiences and inspirations came from watching my mother - from the basics of chopping an onion to making a few of the recipes in this book.

My father used to talk to me about food and drink in the days of the Maharanas, and about the medicinal properties of various ingredients. He himself cooked only a very few dishes but they were always extremely good. He wanted me to go into mechanical engineering, which was his speciality. Being a chef is considered a lowly profession in India and when I chose it as a career my parents had to face a certain amount of mockery from friends to whom chefs were merely domestic hands.

While I was at boarding school I regularly visited an uncle's hotel and this is when I decided to work in catering. After completing a diploma in hotel management I took a job at the Taj Mahal Hotel in Bombay as an apprentice cook. At that time kitchen apprentices were expected to endure the most appalling hardships, including both physical and verbal abuse, and all for a salary that I would be ashamed to offer even the greenest of recruits. But at least it gave me the opportunity to acquire the knowledge and skills I needed. At the same time I also ran my own little bakery from home, often baking until 4am before getting up at 7 to leave for a day's work. I spent almost 15 years with the Taj group, eventually becoming executive chef of its prestigious hotel complex in Goa. My training took place in the Continental kitchens (there was a separate kitchen for Indian food), where I specialized in French cuisine and particularly patisserie and bakery. However, after I moved to Goa I began to take more interest in Indian cooking and to research it thoroughly. I became convinced that what my country had to offer was far greater than the rest of the world's cuisines put together, and that I could never master it in 10 lifetimes.

Indian cuisine is very diverse, with immense regional, cultural and religious variations, and can be as simple or as intricate as you like. Dating back long before the earliest European cuisines were established, it is no wonder that over the centuries it has acquired a scientific and medical dimension. Because of India's inhospitable climate, ways of preserving food with herbs and spices were developed and this eventually led to an understanding of their medicinal uses - the science known as Ayurveda. It was also discovered that certain combinations of foods and spices create a balance and eliminate unpleasant side effects, and so a dietary approach to health was established. Long before Hippocrates said in 330 BC, 'Let food be thy medicine.' Vedic philosophy quite simply stated, 'You are what you eat.'

After I left the Taj group I planned to emigrate to Australia but an old friend asked me to help him run a restaurant in London instead. Somehow London felt like home. There seemed to be tremendous opportunites for chefs – and scope for a new style of Indian restaurant. In 1991 I became executive chef at the Namaste restaurant, then in 1995 I opened the first Café Spice Namaste with my business partner Michael Gottlieb. We wanted the restaurant to reflect India's true nature: bright, vibrant, colourful, creative and above all diverse. India is often described as a nation that embodies unity in its diversity. It is a fusion of cultures, religions, languages and people from all walks of life, living together in harmony. The philosophy behind our restaurant is to let customers experience that variety through the food of the subcontinent, and we always feature authentic regional dishes on the menu – especially those of Goa and the Parsee community, my two main culinary influences. We pride ourselves on creating a friendly and welcoming atmosphere. *Namaste*, incidentally, means a gracious hello and welcome.

There is no place quite like the UK today for food. It offers a huge variety of ingredients from India and every other part of the world and I would urge you to cast off any inhibitions and start experimenting with them. I am constantly stimulated by the produce at my disposal to create new dishes, some of which are featured in this book, such as Ostrich Tikka Toofan Mail (see page 72) and Crocodile Ambotik (see page 79).

Although Indian restaurants are extraordinarily popular in the UK, the complexity of the cooking (and the unfamiliarity of some of the ingredients) deters many people from trying it at home. However, most of the recipes I have included in this book are quite simple to prepare. If you prefer, use them as a guideline and adjust them to suit yourself as you go along. That is the best way to learn about food, and Indian dishes vary from household to household in any case. Don't be afraid of making mistakes: these are easygoing, forgiving dishes that can easily be put right or adapted with a little bit of imagination. Very few of them require the sort of precision that you would need to make a soufflé, for example. What is important is to taste as you go along, paying particular attention to the balance of flavours.

Planning an Indian meal is not as complex as some people fear, as long as you ensure that the food is well balanced. A lentil dish, for instance, should not be served alongside a chick pea one, as both can cause flatulence. A creamy dish should be accompanied by light vegetables, preferably greens. Rice or wholemeal breads are generally preferable to heavier, richer breads (although Parsees or staunch Muslims may think otherwise). Always serve a fried dish with curry and rice and a good *cachumber* or salad with plenty of sliced onions to help digestion. In India pickles and *papads* are traditionally eaten with the main course, not served as an appetizer as they are in the UK. Make a habit of this when having an Indian meal and you will find that you relish the food much more.

These are just a few guidelines; with practice you will find that putting a menu together comes easily. If you are relaxed about the planning and keep it simple, you can't go far wrong.

Starters, Snacks
and Finger Foods

Badal Jaam

AUBERGINE SLICES WITH TOMATO SAUCE AND A TANGY YOGHURT DRESSING

Heat a few tablespoons of the oil in a frying pan and fry the aubergine slices (in batches if necessary) until well browned on both sides. Arrange them on a baking tray without overlapping.

Give the tomatoes a quick whirl in a blender until roughly chopped. If using canned tomatoes, drain and mash coarsely with a potato masher to make a thick, spreadable sauce.

Heat the remaining oil in the pan in which the aubergines were fried. Add the onion and fry until light brown. Stir in the ginger and garlic (keeping aside a teaspoon of the garlic for the dressing) and fry until golden. Then add the chilli powder, tomatoes and some salt and simmer until the mixture has a thick, saucelike consistency. Stir in half the coriander, check the seasoning and add a sprinkling of fenugreek if you like.

Sprinkle *chaat masala* on the aubergine slices and spoon tomato sauce on each one. Cover with foil and place in an oven preheated to 140°C/275°F/Gas Mark 1 for 5–10 minutes, until heated through. Meanwhile, make the topping: whisk the yoghurt until smooth. Stir in the reserved garlic, the remaining coriander and the lemon juice.

Transfer the aubergine slices to a serving platter and top each one with a dollop of the yoghurt dressing.

5–6 tbsp oil

2 long aubergines or 1 broad one, cut into rounds 5 mm thick

500 g tomatoes (or 400 g can of tomatoes)

1 onion, finely chopped

2 cm piece of fresh ginger root, finely chopped

8–10 garlic cloves, finely chopped

1/2 tsp chilli powder

2 tbsp chopped fresh coriander

toasted fenugreek leaves (see below), to taste (optional)

chaat masala, for sprinkling

500 g Greek-style yoghurt

1 tbsp lemon juice

salt

VARIATION
You can sprinkle on top some deep-fried egg noodles or *sev*. You can even top it with *chewda*, also known as Bombay mix.

TO TOAST FENUGREEK
This improves and mellows the flavour of dried fenugreek. Preheat the oven to 150°C/200°F/Gas Mark 2. Spread out a packet of dried fenugreek leaves on a baking tray, put them in the oven and then switch off the oven. Leave for 4–5 hours. The fenugreek will become lightly toasted. Pick out the stems, then crumble the fenugreek finely between your fingers. You could also try toasting it in a warm airing cupboard. Use as desired and store in an airtight jar for future use.

Perhaps the most popular Indian snack in the UK and also the most misunderstood. The product available in shops and supermarkets does not even vaguely resemble the *bhajia* that would be made in an Indian home. Try this recipe. It is very simple and the results will astound you.

Onion Bhajia

MAKES 12-14

2 onions, sliced as thinly as possible

2 green chillies, finely chopped

1/2 tsp chilli powder

2 tbsp chopped fresh coriander

1/2 tsp lemon juice

1 tsp cumin seeds, crushed

1/2 tsp ajwain (carom seeds), crushed

6-7 tbsp besan (chick pea flour)

1/2 tsp salt, or to taste

oil for deep-frying

2 tbsp water

Put the onions in a large bowl and add the green chillies, chilli powder, fresh coriander, lemon juice, cumin and *ajwain*. Sift the chick pea flour with the salt.

Heat plenty of oil in a *kadhai*-type container or a deep pan but do not let it get too hot.

Gradually add the sifted flour to the onion mixture, rubbing it in with your fingers until firm and sticky. Add the water and mix well. With your already messy fingers, put small dollops of the mixture into the oil to fry - just a few at a time or they will be soggy. The *bhajia* should be no bigger than 2.5 cm. Do not make the sort of tennis balls you might be used to seeing elsewhere! Fry them slowly until crisp and golden on the outside and cooked through in the centre - about 3-4 minutes. If the oil is too hot they will be raw and gooey inside.

Drain in a sieve placed over a bowl and then serve immediately, with Green Chutney (see page 25), Green Coconut Chutney (see page 36) or Fresh Tomato Chutney (see page 119).

BHAJEE (BHAJI) AND *BHAJIA* - WHAT IS THE DIFFERENCE?
In restaurants and shops in the UK these terms are used almost interchangeably but in fact they refer to two very different dishes and should not be confused. A *bhajee* (or *bhaji*) is vegetables cooked in a sauce, whereas a *bhajia* is a fritter.

This can be garnished with hard-boiled eggs or olives, if you like.

Shinanio Chi Salade

MUSSEL COCKTAIL

Scrub the mussels well under cold running water and pull out the beards. Discard any open mussels that do not close when tapped on a work surface.

Heat the oil in a large pan, add the onion or shallots, garlic and carrot and fry gently until the onion is translucent. Increase the heat to high, add the mussels and green chilli and sauté for 2-3 minutes. Now add the wine and some salt. Cover the pan and cook until the shells have opened. This should not take more than 2 minutes or so. Remove from the heat and leave to cool in the pan.

Remove the mussels from the pan, scraping any of the chopped ingredients back into the pan. Discard any mussels whose shells have not opened. Remove the meat from the shells and either discard the shells or keep the lower half of each shell if you want to present the mussels in them. Cover the mussels tightly when cool and keep them in the fridge until ready to serve.

Discard the chilli. Reheat the vegetable mixture in the pan and simmer it until the liquid has evaporated. Leave to cool and then stir it into the mayonnaise, with the paprika, a little at a time until you are happy with the flavour. Mix in the coriander and your dressing is ready.

Fold the mussels into the dressing. Now you can either shred the lettuce leaves and mix them with the mussels to make a cocktail; spoon each mussel into a half shell; or arrange them on a bed of lettuce.

24 medium or 36 small mussels

1 tbsp olive oil

1 onion or 4-5 shallots, finely chopped

2-3 garlic cloves, finely chopped

1 small carrot, finely diced or chopped

1 large green chilli, slit open and deseeded

$^1/_2$ glass of dry white wine

2 heaped tbsp mayonnaise (preferably home-made, see page 113)

$^1/_4$-$^1/_2$ tsp paprika

2 tsp chopped fresh coriander

mixed lettuce leaves, to serve

salt

This recipe is very versatile. You can substitute oysters, mussels or any other shellfish for the scallops, or even a firm-fleshed fish such as monkfish, shark, tuna or swordfish. The mixture can also be used as a delicious omelette filling.

Adrak Lehsun Aur Mirch Kay Scallop

SCALLOPS WITH GINGER, GARLIC AND CHILLI

20-30 fresh queen scallops
1 tbsp oil
1 tbsp finely chopped fresh ginger root
6 garlic cloves, finely chopped
1-2 green chillies, chopped
½ tsp ground cumin
½ tsp ground coriander
½ tsp ground turmeric
½ tbsp finely chopped fresh coriander
salt

Drain the scallops and leave them in the colander or sieve until you are ready to cook them.

Heat the oil in a heavy-based frying pan until it is almost at smoking point. Put in the scallops and spread them out evenly. Immediately add the ginger, garlic and chillies. Toss and level out again. Don't stir, as this will reduce the temperature in the pan, causing the scallops to give off their juices and become rubbery.

Toss again and add the ground spices. Stir briefly to mix everything, then taste and add salt if necessary. Toss in the fresh coriander.

The scallops should be cooked for no longer than 3-4 minutes; I prefer them cooked for only 2 minutes.

Serve immediately, with the juices that the scallops will now have given off. Toasted brioche and green salad make good accompaniments.

TIP
Coriander is a delicate herb and must be chopped carefully with a very sharp knife. If you go over it repeatedly with the knife, as for chopping parsley, it will bruise and turn black.

A simple yet delicious chicken dish. It can be made in minutes and will delight your guests. Prawns, mussels, baby sweetcorn and slender French beans can all be substituted for the chicken. Adjust the cooking time as necessary but remember that the minimum of cooking will yield the best results.

Jeera Murg

CHICKEN WITH CUMIN

250 g boneless chicken, cut into 1-cm dice

1 tsp lemon juice

1-1½ tbsp oil

2 tsp cumin seeds, roasted and lightly crushed (see below)

2 tsp chopped fresh coriander

salt

Sprinkle the chicken with the lemon juice and some salt. Heat the oil in a heavy-based pan until it almost reaches smoking point, then put in the chicken and crushed cumin. Keep the flame high and swirl the chicken around, but not too often. This cools the pan down a little and allows the moisture from the chicken to escape. Toss for 2-3 minutes, until the chicken is cooked through, then taste and add more salt if necessary. Sprinkle with the coriander and serve.

TO ROAST CUMIN OR CORIANDER SEEDS
Put the seeds in a heavy-based frying pan and set the pan over a low heat. Keep shaking the pan until the seeds are well roasted but not burnt. Crush them lightly in a mortar and pestle. They keep very well in a tightly sealed jar and can be used in many dishes.
Roasted crushed cumin is excellent for heartburn or an acidic stomach. Just chew some with a little sugar.

This method of cooking game birds was a particular favourite of the Maharanas of Oudh, better known as Avadh. Boned quails are readily available now from supermarkets and some butchers.

Dudhia Bataer

QUAILS FRIED IN MILK BATTER

Put the milk in a deep pan and add the peppercorns, fennel, cardamom pods, bay leaves, saffron, cinnamon and some salt. Bring to the boil, add the quails, then reduce the heat and simmer until tender – about 8 minutes. Remove the quails from the pan and leave to cool. Simmer the milk until reduced to about 150 ml. Strain, discarding the spices, and leave to cool. Do not worry if the milk separates. The reduction will have a good flavour.

For the batter, put all the ingredients in a bowl and whisk together with enough of the reduced milk to give a fairly thick consistency.

Heat some *ghee* or oil for deep-frying. Cut the quails in half lengthways and check the seasoning. Dip each quail half into the batter and fry briefly until golden brown. Do not allow them to brown too much or they will become tough. Drain on kitchen paper and serve straight away, with a salad.

You may like to serve Green Chutney (see page 25) or Fresh Tomato Chutney (see page 119) along with it.

SERVES 6

500 ml milk

5-6 black peppercorns, roughly crushed

1 tsp fennel seeds

6-8 green cardamom pods

1-2 bay leaves

a few saffron strands (use only good Mancha or pure Kashmiri saffron)

2-cm piece of cinnamon stick

6 boned quails

ghee or oil for deep-frying

salt

For the batter:

50 g besan (chick pea flour)

$\frac{1}{4}$ tsp ground fennel seed

$\frac{1}{4}$ tsp chilli powder

1 tsp sugar

1 tbsp lemon juice

a few saffron strands

1 egg (optional – it gives a lighter batter)

salt

Liver is treated as a delicacy in India. This simple recipe uses plenty of fresh coriander and mint, which really enhances the flavour of chicken livers. Serve with soft scrambled eggs and toast or with hot *chapatis*. Lamb's or calf's liver can be cooked in the same way but should be finely diced first.

Masala Ma Tatraveli Kaleji

SAUTÉED CHICKEN LIVERS WITH CORIANDER AND MINT

250 g chicken livers

2-cm piece of fresh ginger root, very finely chopped

6 garlic cloves, very finely chopped

1 large green chilli, very finely chopped

¼ tsp ground turmeric

½ tsp ground cumin

juice of ½ lemon

2 tbsp oil

2½ tbsp chopped fresh coriander

1½ tbsp chopped fresh mint

salt

Clean the chicken livers and cut them in half. Mix together the ginger, garlic, chilli, turmeric, cumin, lemon juice and some salt and then stir this mixture into the chicken livers until they are thoroughly coated.

Heat the oil to smoking point in a large heavy-based frying pan, then add the livers. Don't stir them too much; just shake the pan to toss them or stir very lightly with a wooden spatula. Cook for 4–5 minutes, until browned on the outside but still pink inside, or longer if you prefer them well done. Toss in the coriander and mint, then check the seasoning, adding a squeeze of lemon juice if you like, and serve immediately.

Idlis are one of India's greatest snack or breakfast foods. Though southern Indian in origin, they have become popular throughout the country. The traditional recipe takes 24 hours to make but here is a quick and easy version - a speciality of my wife, Pervin. If you don't have an *idli* dish (available from southern Indian food shops) for steaming the cakes you can improvise with an ordinary cake tin, although the *idli* will not be as light.

Instant Rava Idli

INSTANT SEMOLINA CAKES

Mix the semolina and yoghurt together, then stir in the spring onion, tomato, chillies and coriander.

Heat the oil in a small frying pan until very hot. Add one or two mustard seeds to check that the oil is hot enough: they should crackle. Add all the mustard seeds, then when they start to crackle, add the curry leaves and lastly the asafoetida. Remove from the heat, cool slightly, then pour into the yoghurt and semolina mixture straight from the pan. Stir in the fruit salts.

If you are using an *idli* steamer, grease the dish with oil or butter and bring about 1-2 cm of water to the boil in the pan. Pour in the batter, up to the top of each small mould, and steam for about 10 minutes, until the mixture feels spongy and doesn't stick to your fingers.

If you don't have an *idli* steamer, pour all the batter into a greased shallow cake tin and steam it in an ordinary steamer for about 20 minutes. Cut into wedges to serve.

Once unmoulded, the *idli* can be kept warm wrapped in a cloth. They can also be reheated by steaming again if necessary, enclosed, or wrapped loosely in a cloth.

180-200g semolina

150 ml yoghurt

1 spring onion, finely chopped

1 tomato, deseeded and finely chopped

2 green chillies, finely chopped

1 tbsp chopped fresh coriander

2 tbsp oil

½ tsp mustard seeds

2-4 curry leaves, finely shredded

a large pinch of asafoetida

1 tsp fruit salts (such as Eno's or Andrew's)

VARIATION
The *idli* can be stuffed with left-over cooked mince or Green Coconut Chutney (see page 36) for an inventive variation. Pour half the mixture into the dish or mould, add the filling, then cover with the remaining mixture and steam as usual.

This stuffed, rolled *chapati* used to be Bombay's best-selling street snack until it was overtaken by modern American-style fast food. However, it is still a favourite with many.

Frankie

MAKES 8

3 eggs

chilli powder (optional)

oil, ghee or butter for frying

8 plain chapatis or flour tortillas

2 onions, sliced

1 tbsp chopped fresh coriander

10 mint leaves, coarsely chopped

salt

For the filling:

2 tbsp oil

500 g boned leg of lamb, cut into 1-cm dice

2 onions, very finely chopped

2 tbsp Ginger/Garlic Paste (see page 61)

1 tbsp ground coriander

1 tsp ground cumin

1 tbsp red chilli paste (see below)

4-5 tbsp Greek-style yoghurt

1-2 tomatoes, chopped (optional)

1 tbsp lemon juice

1 tsp garam masala (see page 123)

2 tbsp chopped fresh coriander

1 tbsp chopped fresh mint

salt

To make the filling, heat the oil in a casserole, add the lamb and cook over a medium-high heat until the meat is browned and any liquid has dried out. Add the onions, ginger/garlic paste, coriander, cumin and chilli paste. Sauté until the onions and spices start to turn a rich, dark colour, stirring and scraping the bottom of the pan frequently. Season with salt, then reduce the heat, cover and cook for 15-20 minutes, stirring frequently to prevent sticking. If the mixture dries out too quickly, stir in a couple of tablespoons of water.

Stir in the yoghurt and the tomatoes, if using, then cover and continue to cook until the lamb is tender and a thick, rich-looking gravy has formed. Add the lemon juice, *garam masala*, coriander and mint, then cover and set aside. If necessary, remove any excess oil floating on the top (save it to use in other lamb dishes).

Beat the eggs well with 3 tablespoons of water. Add salt and, if you like, some chilli powder. Heat a *tawa* or griddle over a medium heat. Coat it with a teaspoon of oil or brush with a little *ghee* or butter. Put a *chapati* or flour tortilla on the pan and pour a little egg on the top, spreading it over the bread with the back of a spoon. As soon as the egg coagulates, flip the bread over and coat the other side. When both sides are golden brown, remove from the pan. Place a tablespoon or two of the lamb mixture on top, sprinkle with sliced onion, chopped coriander and mint, then roll up and serve. Repeat with the remaining *chapatis* or tortillas.

TIP

To make your own red chilli paste, snip a handful of red chillies into pieces, then soak in about 150 ml water until swollen and soft. Purée in a blender with the soaking liquid to make a thick paste. Store in the refrigerator.

I was taught to prepare these by the mother of the managing director of the Taj hotel group. Serve with a fresh green chutney, such as the one on page 25 or page 36, or tomato ketchup spiced up with some chopped green chilli and a little chopped fresh coriander. Spring roll pastry is available in most Asian food shops. If you cannot get it you could substitute filo, although this absorbs more oil when fried.

Goan Prawn Samosas

Wash the prawns and drain well, ensuring there is no moisture left. Chop them very finely or mince them. Pound the cumin and coriander seeds to a coarse powder in a mortar and pestle. Heat the oil in a pan and sauté the chopped onions until softened, then add the ginger, garlic and green chillies. Add the cumin and coriander, stir for a minute or two, then raise the heat to high and add the prawns. Stir well to break up lumps and cook for 2–3 minutes, until any liquid has evaporated. Season with salt to taste and stir in the lemon juice and chopped coriander. Transfer the mixture to a plate and leave to cool.

Place a 23-cm plate upside down over the pile of spring roll pastry sheets and cut round it with a knife to give 8 circles of pastry. (Either discard the trimmings or cut them into small pieces and deep-fry them later for a delightful snack when mixed with a salad - see *Chaats*, pages 30–31). Cut the stack of dough rounds in half to make semi-circles, then peel off the sheets in pairs. Keep them covered with a cloth while you make the samosas or they will become dry and brittle.

Take one of the double-thickness semi-circles and fold over one-third, then apply beaten egg or flour and water paste along the edge to seal. Fold over the other third to form a cone and seal the edge again. Open up the top and put in just over a tablespoon of the filling. Seal the opening with the egg or paste and press well together, ensuring that there are no gaps. Sometimes there is a little hole at the bottom tip, so seal this if necessary. Prepare the remaining samosas in the same way.

Heat some oil in a large pan and deep-fry the samosas over a medium heat for 2–3 minutes or until golden. Drain on paper towels and serve.

MAKES 8

250–300 g shelled raw prawns

1 tsp cumin seeds

1 tsp coriander seeds

4 tbsp oil

2 onions, very finely chopped

2-cm piece of fresh ginger root, very finely chopped

6–8 garlic cloves, very finely chopped

3–4 green chillies (deseeded if you like), very finely chopped

1½ tsp lemon juice

2–3 tbsp chopped fresh coriander

8 large sheets of spring roll pastry

beaten egg or flour and water paste, to seal

oil for deep-frying

salt

The *tamota ni gravy*, or tomato sauce, keeps well, covered, in the fridge and is excellent with croquettes, fried fish or chicken. For extra flavour you can include fresh green chillies, slit open lengthwise (otherwise they might explode in the pan), and a few cloves, putting them in with the dried red chillies.

Machchi Na Pattice
Nay Tamota Ni Gravy

250 g white fish fillets, skinned

1 large green chilli, chopped

2-cm piece of fresh ginger root, chopped

6-8 garlic cloves, chopped

2 tbsp chopped fresh coriander

1 tsp salt

1 tbsp lemon juice

1 egg

2 slices of white bread, soaked in water for a few seconds, then squeezed out thoroughly

For the Tamota Ni Gravy:

2-3 tbsp oil

2 pieces of cinnamon stick

2 large dried red chillies, broken into 3-4 pieces each

2 small to medium onions, finely chopped

1 heaped tbsp Ginger/Garlic Paste (see page 61)

5 tomatoes, chopped, or 400 g-can of chopped tomatoes

1 tbsp malt vinegar

1 tbsp grated jaggery

1½ tsp prepared tamarind pulp (see page 28) or paste, or ½ tsp concentrate (optional)

salt

For frying the fish cakes:

100 g plain flour

2-3 eggs

oil

FISH CAKES WITH TOMATO SAUCE

First make the sauce. Heat the oil in a casserole, add the cinnamon sticks and sauté until swollen and deep brown in colour but not burnt. Add the chillies and cook for 15-20 seconds, then add the onions. Sauté until they are softened but not browned. Add the ginger/garlic paste and sauté for a further minute or so, then stir in the tomatoes. Add the vinegar, jaggery and tamarind, if using, then cover and simmer for 15-20 minutes, stirring occasionally, until thick and saucelike. Taste and add salt if necessary.

Next prepare the fish cakes. Put all the ingredients in a food processor and process until well combined. Taste and add more salt if necessary. (If you prefer not to taste the raw mixture, fry a small piece and taste it. Don't make the fish cakes until you have approved the taste for yourself.) Divide the mixture into 8 balls. Spread the flour out in a tray big enough to hold all the fish cakes. Beat the eggs thoroughly in a shallow bowl or soup plate. Pour enough oil into a frying pan to fill it to a depth of about 5 mm and set it over a medium heat. Flatten each ball to about 1-1.5 cm thick, smoothing the edges so that they are not jagged or uneven. Dip each fish cake into the flour, then into the egg, allowing excess egg to run off, and then place in the hot oil. Raise the heat if the oil begins to foam. If you want the fish cakes to have a frilly appearance, make sure the eggs are well beaten and fry the fish cakes straight away. Fry for a few minutes, turning once, until golden brown on both sides, then transfer to a tray lined with kitchen paper to drain.

Serve with the tomato sauce. The fish cakes can also be eaten cold, stuffed in small bread rolls as a snack.

A simple yet surprisingly variable egg dish. My mother taught me to make it and she makes the best I have ever had. Serve with mango chutney and soft bread. In India we have gorgeous breads. One of the most common is *ladi pao*, meaning tray bread. This is similar to batch-baked rolls but, unlike the ones available in the UK, contains no preservatives or improvers, which make the bread unnaturally light. *Pain rustique* or warm baguette are also good with this dish.

Papeta Pur Eeda

EGGS ON POTATOES

2-3 tbsp oil
1 tsp cumin seeds
1 small green chilli, finely chopped
2 garlic cloves, finely chopped
1 onion, finely sliced
1 large potato, peeled and cut into slices about 3 mm thick
1 tbsp finely chopped fresh coriander
4 eggs
salt

Heat the oil in a large frying pan, add the cumin seeds and allow them to sizzle for a minute. Add the green chilli and garlic and sauté for a minute or two. Add the onion and sauté for a few minutes, until translucent, then add the potato slices. Cook for 3-4 minutes, without letting them brown, then sprinkle with salt and level out the mixture. Pour in enough water to come just below the contents of the pan, cover and cook over a low heat until the potato is tender but not mushy. Sprinkle with the coriander, check the seasoning, then mix gently by folding everything in a slow motion and levelling it out again.

Make sure the sides of the pan are clean. Use an egg to make 4 indentations in the mixture, well spaced out. They should be roughly 4 cm from the side of the pan. Break an egg into each indentation, making sure the yolk goes in it, then cover the pan and cook on a very low heat. The eggs will poach in the steam.

When done to your liking, (I prefer my yolk soft), cut into 4 segments and serve with mango chutney and bread.

Papeta Na Pattice

POTATO CAKES

2 large floury potatoes such as
King Edward (weighing about
450 g in total), peeled and
chopped

1 tbsp chopped fresh coriander

1-2 green chillies, finely chopped

1 tsp chaat masala

½ tsp ground cumin

1 tsp lemon juice

1 tsp salt, or to taste

cornflour

oil for frying

a little sugar

For the topping:

1 large potato, boiled, peeled and
diced

1 onion, chopped

2 tbsp chopped fresh coriander

chaat masala, for sprinkling

Boil the potatoes until tender. Drain well and return the pan to a very low heat. Dry the potato out in the pan by stirring continuously with a wooden spoon, scraping the bottom of the pan. After all that stirring the potatoes probably won't need mashing; just break up any lumps that remain.

Mix the potatoes with the coriander, chillies, *chaat masala*, cumin, lemon juice and salt, working the mixture to a pliable dough with your hands. If it seems too moist, add some cornflour until it is dry enough not to stick to your palms. Check the seasoning and then divide the mixture into balls about 3-4 cm in diameter. If you have kneaded the dough well the balls should have a smooth edge and will not crack when flattened. If they do crack, smooth the edges.

Pour some oil into a large frying pan to a depth of about 1-1.5cm and set it over a medium heat. Spread some cornflour on a large plate and roll the potato balls in it to coat. Flatten them to about 1-1.5cm thick, shake off excess cornflour and fry them in the hot oil until well browned. Remove from the pan and drain on kitchen paper.

Serve in one of the following suggested ways: with a raita (see page 118); with a simple Ragda (see page 104) and small bread rolls; with a chutney such as Tamarind and Date Chutney (see opposite) for a quick snack; or with tomato ketchup that has chopped chilli, garlic and fresh coriander stirred into it.

VARIATIONS
• Roll the pattice in finely chopped peanuts or cashew nuts instead of cornflour. This will give a nice nutty flavour and is more interesting, but do make sure that none of your guests is allergic to nuts.

• Stuff the pattice with nuts, green chutney, green peas, grated paneer, cottage cheese, ricotta or sautéed prawns - try the filling for Goan Prawn Samosas on page 19.

This is one of Bombay's all-time-great snacks, and thousands of portions are sold there daily. If you have everything ready in advance it can be assembled in a matter of minutes. The chutneys keep well in a sealed jar in the fridge so it is worth making up a large amount.

Sev Batata Poorie

CRISPY POORIES WITH CHICK PEA VERMICELLI AND POTATOES

To make the poories, sift the wholemeal flour, rice flour and salt into a bowl, then stir in the semolina. Warm the oil slightly, then stir it into the mixture. Gradually add enough water to make a firm dough (about the same consistency as pasta dough). Knead until smooth, then cover and set aside for an hour.

Meanwhile, prepare the chutneys. For the tamarind chutney, bring 200 ml water to the boil in a saucepan, then add the tamarind, dates and jaggery and simmer for about 20 minutes, until the dates are soft. Leave to cool, then purée and season to taste with salt.

For the green chutney, just purée all the ingredients in a blender, adding enough water to make a thick paste. Check the seasoning, adding a little more sugar if necessary.

Divide the *poorie* dough into 4 pieces and roll out each piece very thinly - it should be a little less than 2 mm thick. Cut out rounds with a 4-cm pastry cutter. Pour some oil into a *karahi* or wok to a depth of 2-3 cm and place over a medium heat (if it is too hot the dough will puff, which is not ideal for this recipe). Fry the *poorie*, a few at a time, for ½-1 minute, until golden brown. They will sink to the bottom of the oil at first, then rise to the top when they are about done. Drain well and leave to cool.

To assemble everything, place 12 poories on a platter (any extra ones can be stored in an airtight container lined with kitchen paper). Top them with the potato, then the onion and then the coriander. Sprinkle with *chaat masala*. Top each *poorie* with the chutneys - about a teaspoon of each or a bit less. Next sprinkle the *sev* and coriander on top. Serve immediately.

250 g wholemeal flour

60 g rice flour

1 tsp salt

60 g semolina

4 tbsp oil, plus oil for frying

sev and chopped fresh coriander, to garnish

For the tamarind and date chutney:

1 tbsp tamarind concentrate or 2 tbsp tamarind paste

8-10 dates, stoned

25 g jaggery

salt

For the green chutney:

15 g fresh mint leaves

15 g fresh coriander

3-4 green chillies

½ tsp salt

3-4 garlic cloves

1 tsp cumin seeds

2 tsp lemon juice

a little sugar

For the topping:

1 large potato, boiled and diced

1 onion, chopped

2 tbsp chopped fresh coriander

chaat masala, for sprinkling

This is a Parsee speciality from Gujerat. Parsees love eggs and often include this type of omelette in their picnics or use it as a filling stuffed into *chapatis*. It is like a Spanish omelette except it has more spices and no potato.

Bhujelo Poro

BAKED SPICY OMELETTE

2 slender green chillies

3 garlic cloves

1-2-cm piece of fresh ginger root

1 tbsp chopped fresh coriander

½ tsp cumin seeds

¼ tsp salt

a pinch of ground turmeric

2 egg yolks

4 egg whites

1 teaspoon plain flour

1 tsp ghee or clarified butter

Put the chillies, garlic, ginger, coriander, cumin, salt and turmeric in a mortar and grind to a fine paste (or use a blender, adding a very little water if necessary). Lightly beat the egg yolks, then stir in the spice paste. Beat the egg whites until stiff, then gently fold in the egg yolk mixture and the flour.

Heat the *ghee* or clarified butter in a 20-cm ovenproof frying pan until very hot. Add the omelette mixture and leave on the heat for a few seconds, then transfer the pan to the centre of an oven preheated to 220°C/425°F/Gas Mark 7 and bake until the omelette is well risen, light and fluffy. It shouldn't take longer than 5 minutes. Serve immediately, with warm bread, such as good *pain rustique*, or toast and a sweet chutney.

TIP
When selecting root ginger, look for a smooth piece with as few knots as possible.

This is another Parsee speciality and, like several of their dishes, was probably created centuries ago. It is perhaps the most tedious method of cooking scrambled eggs ever invented but I think it is the very best. However, patience is essential.

I would like to make a suggestion that I find very effective (although my mother may not agree). The mixture without the eggs and butter can be kept covered in the refrigerator for months. You can then use it as you wish, adding just one egg or two if you like, and finishing it off with the fresh coriander. It also makes an excellent omelette.

Akoori

SPICY SCRAMBLED EGGS

Heat the oil in a pan and fry the sliced onions in it until crisp and golden (see page 103). Drain and leave on kitchen paper to dry.

Put half the oil back in the pan and reheat gently. Add the ginger, garlic and green chilli and fry until the garlic is golden. Add all the ground spices and continue to cook gently for a minute or two. Add the tomato, stir for a minute and then return the onions to the pan. Add the sultanas, if using (the Parsees of Bharooch in Gujerat love it made with sultanas).

Now stir in the vinegar, lemon juice, sugar and some salt to taste. Remove from the heat and drain off as much oil as you can (save the oil, as it is good to use in other dishes). Add the butter and eggs and beat them into the mixture. Return to a very low heat and cook very slowly, stirring continuously, to achieve a creamy, scrambled texture. Add the fresh coriander and check the seasoning. Serve with toast or warm *pain rustique*.

6 tbsp oil

2 onions, finely sliced

2-cm piece of fresh ginger root, finely chopped

4 garlic cloves, finely chopped

1 green chilli, finely chopped

3/4 tsp ground cumin

1 tsp ground coriander

a large pinch of ground turmeric

1/2 tsp chilli powder

1 tomato, deseeded and chopped

1 tbsp sultanas (optional)

1 tsp malt vinegar

1/2 tsp lemon juice

1 tsp sugar

15 g butter

6 large eggs

1-2 tbsp chopped fresh coriander

salt

A Maharashtrian salad from the Ratnagiri district, which is on India's west coast, south of Bombay. Roasted salted cashew nuts or almonds can be substituted for the peanuts. A few diced olives can be added to the salad, although this is not authentically Indian.

Tantia Ani Shingdaney Chi Usli

EGG AND PEANUT SALAD

5 eggs

6 tablespoons fresh or thawed frozen grated coconut (see page 96)

1-2 large green chillies, finely chopped

2 tbsp finely chopped fresh coriander

1 tbsp prepared tamarind pulp (see below) or paste, or 1½ tsp concentrate

3-4 tablespoons roasted peanuts, coarsely chopped

salt

Optional extras:

1 tbsp chopped shallots

2 tbsp chopped tomatoes

Hard-boil the eggs by immersing them in boiling water and simmering for 7 minutes. Remove from the heat and cool them in the water by adding a few ice cubes to it. This cools them slowly and ensures that they are cooked through.

Shell the eggs and take out the yolks. Cut the whites into small dice and crumble the yolks roughly with a fork. Mix in all the other ingredients and season to taste. If you are serving the salad immediately, include the shallots and tomatoes.

VARIATION
Flakes of tuna, or *boogdi* as it is known in Goa, make an excellent addition. You can also mix in or serve with lettuce if you like.

TO PREPARE TAMARIND PULP
Ready-to-use tamarind paste and concentrate are now available in Indian food shops and some supermarkets. If using concentrate, you will need to dilute it with water before use.

Tamarind is also available as a compressed block containing the seeds and pulp. To prepare this, soak the block in about 500 ml boiling water for at least 1 hour. Then mash it with your fingers, squeezing out all the pulp from the seeds, and pass it through a sieve, rubbing it through with a spoon. Discard the seeds and fibres left in the sieve and use the pulp as required. It can be stored in a jar in the fridge for some time.

Chaats

Chaat means 'lick' in Hindi, Gujerati and a few other Indian languages. *Chaats* are basically cold finger foods or light salads, whose ingredients vary according to the time of year. They are simple to make and you need only a few ingredients unless you are going for something complicated. The essential seasoning is *chaat masala*, which always contains *amchur* (mango powder), *jeera* (ground cumin) and *kala namak* (black salt). Other ingredients for the *masala* vary, although red chilli is the most common. Your best bet is to buy packets of ready-made *chaat masala*.

Aloo Chaat

POTATO SALAD

1 large or 2 medium potatoes, boiled, peeled and cut into small dice

1 small onion, chopped

1 green chilli, deseeded and chopped

1 tbsp chopped fresh coriander

1 plum tomato, chopped

1 tsp chaat masala, or to taste

The best known of Indian *chaats*, this is very simple to make. Place all the ingredients in a bowl and toss lightly until well combined. Taste and add more *masala* if needed. Serve plain or with Yoghurt, Tamarind and Chilli Dip (see page 114).

VARIATIONS
• Add lettuce or diced fruit such as apple and banana.

• Lightly crush some crispy *poories* or deep-fried flour tortillas and stir them into the *chaat* just before serving.

• Mix with lettuce and cold chicken *tikka* or prawns to make an excellent accompaniment, starter, or snack to serve with drinks.

• Channa Chaat: substitute chick peas for the potatoes, or blend both together

• Cashew Nut Chaat: substitute roasted cashews for the potatoes, or use half potatoes and half nuts. To roast your own cashews, put the nuts into a bowl, pour over boiling water and leave to soak for a minute or two. Drain through a sieve and leave to dry. Rub in 2 tsp oil for every 250 g nuts, then sprinkle with 1 tsp salt per 250 g, or to taste. Mix well. Spread out on a baking tray and roast in an oven preheated to 160-180°C/325-350°F/Gas Mark 3-4 for 40-45 minutes. Stir the nuts regularly and do not let them brown too much. Switch off the oven and leave the nuts to cool in it. Store in an airtight jar for up to a month.

Hara Moong Aur Anar Ki Salaat

GREEN SPROUTED MUNG BEAN AND POMEGRANATE SALAD

Soak 100 g green mung beans in water overnight, then drain and fold them into a kitchen cloth. Dampen the cloth and set it aside in the warmth of your kitchen. Keep the cloth wet at all times. In 2-3 days you should have sprouts just big enough for the salad. Mix the sprouts with the ingredients for Aloo Chaat (see opposite), plus the seeds of 2 pomegranates.

I like to add 3-4 heaped tablespoons of sweetcorn to this *chaat*. It is delicious served in a toasted pitta bread with some soft cheese or *paneer*.

Fruit Chaat

In India fruit *chaats* are very popular in summer. Any diced fruit can be tossed with *chaat masala*, although bananas, apples, papayas, melons, pomegranates and oranges are especially good. Sometimes chopped fresh coriander is added. Serve fruit *chaats* straight away.

Fish and Seafood

A classic recipe. When you want to have a great meal, serve this with my all-time favourite dish, Dhan Daar Nay Vaghaar (see page 103). Pomfret is the best fish to use, although plaice and coley are also good.

Masala Ma Tareli Machchi

PARSEE FISH FRIED IN MASALA

Rub the fish fillets with the turmeric and some salt and set aside for half an hour. Mix together all the remaining ingredients except the oil to make a paste, then taste and check the seasoning. Rub the paste on to the fish, then taste again, sprinkling on more lemon juice or salt if necessary. Place in the refrigerator if you are not cooking it straight away.

Heat a little oil in a large frying pan, add the fish and cook until well coloured underneath before turning it over. Do not let the oil get too hot or the coating will burn very rapidly. When ready, the fish should be crisp outside and delicately soft inside.

VARIATION
After rubbing the paste on to the fish you can dust the fillets in flour, coat them in egg and then in semolina (or just dip them in egg). Deep-fry as you would a crumbed fillet of fish.

about 400 g white fish fillet, cut into 8 pieces about 10 cm long

$\frac{1}{4}$ tsp ground turmeric

1 tbsp lemon juice

1 tsp chilli powder

1 tsp ground cumin

1 tsp ground coriander

$1\frac{1}{2}$ tsp Ginger/Garlic Paste (see page 61)

oil for shallow-frying

salt

A simple curry that does not need a great deal of preparation. Pomfret gives the best flavour but you could substitute other fish such as halibut, cod, kingfish or monkfish.

Leeli Machchi Ni Curry

GREEN FISH CURRY

2 tbsp oil

1 onion, finely sliced

6 garlic cloves, crushed

4-cm piece of fresh ginger root, crushed

2 green chillies, deseeded and finely chopped

½ tsp ground turmeric

400-ml can of coconut milk

4 green cardamom pods

4 cloves

5-6 curry leaves

2-cm piece of cinnamon stick

2 tbsp chopped fresh coriander

4 large fish steaks

salt

Heat the oil in a large pan, add the onion and sauté for a few minutes, until translucent. Add the garlic, ginger and green chillies and cook for 2 minutes, taking care not to let them brown. Stir in the turmeric and cook for a few seconds, then pour in the coconut milk. Bring slowly to the boil, stirring right from the bottom of the mixture. Add some salt, then the cardamom, cloves, curry leaves and cinnamon. Simmer for a couple of minutes, until the mixture has thickened slightly, then add the coriander and cook for a further minute or two. Add the fish and cook for 2–4 minutes, depending on the thickness of the steaks, then cover the pan, remove from the heat and set aside for about 5 minutes. The fish will continue to cook in the heat of the curry. Serve with fried *papads* (papadums) and plain rice or a light *pulao*.

This traditional Parsee dish is very popular at weddings and on other festive occasions. Banana leaves are available in Thai food shops and some Indian ones. If you cannot find them, substitute aluminium foil, although the flavour will not be the same. You can also use a whole fish instead of steaks if you prefer. The chutney is good in sandwiches and with a wide range of snacks.

Patrani Machchi

about 600 g pomfret steaks, cut 2 cm thick (about 3 per person), or 4 halibut steaks

½ tsp ground turmeric

1 packet of banana leaves

malt vinegar for sprinkling

salt

For the green coconut chutney:

250 g fresh or thawed frozen grated coconut (see page 96) or 150 g coconut powder

1 bunch of fresh coriander (the large bunches available from Indian shops, not a supermarket packet)

1 bunch of fresh mint (again, from Indian shops)

4-5 green chillies

6-8 garlic cloves

1 heaped tsp cumin seeds

1 tbsp sugar

juice of 1 large lime, or to taste

salt

FISH IN BANANA LEAF WITH GREEN COCONUT CHUTNEY

Rub the fish with the turmeric and some salt and set aside while you make the chutney. Put all the ingredients for the chutney in a blender and process to a thick paste, adding a little water if necessary. Taste and adjust the seasoning, adding more lime juice if you like. Coat the fish with the coconut chutney on both sides.

Remove the stems from the banana leaves and string the sides (just like stringing green beans). Cut them into squares big enough to wrap the fish steaks in. To make them supple, run each piece over a burner or hot plate until it changes colour and becomes soft. Do not overdo it; just passing it over the heat once on each side should be sufficient.

Wrap each piece of fish in a banana leaf and then tie with string (you can use the strings from the banana leaves).

Place the fish parcels on a baking tray containing about 3 mm water, sprinkle a little vinegar over them, and then place in an oven preheated to 190°C/375°F/Gas Mark 5 for 20 minutes. Remove the strings and serve the fish in the banana leaf.

Fish curry is synonymous with Goa. It is a staple part of the diet and the vast majority of Goans cannot do without it. Serve with Arborio or Camargue rice or with plain steamed long grain rice. It is also good eaten cold or slightly warm the next day, with ciabatta or any crusty bread.

Goan Fish Curry

500 g pomfret steaks or chunky pieces of fillet (or use other firm white fish such as coley, cod or tilapia)

$^1/_4$ tsp ground turmeric

5 tbsp oil

1 onion, finely sliced

2-cm piece of fresh ginger root, finely shredded

2 green chillies, finely shredded

300 ml water or fish stock

4 tbsp prepared tamarind pulp (see page 28) or paste, or $1^1/_2$ tbsp concentrate

2–3 cokums (or 1 tart plum)

salt

For the masala:

50 g dried red chillies (select large ones with a deep colour)

2 tsp coriander seeds

1 tsp cumin seeds

6–8 garlic cloves

4-cm piece of fresh ginger root

$^1/_2$ tsp ground turmeric

250 g fresh or frozen grated coconut (see page 96) or 150 g coconut powder

Put all the ingredients for the *masala* into a blender and mix to a smooth, thick paste, adding only enough water to process the mixture: it should not be runny.

Sprinkle the fish with the turmeric and some salt and set aside. Pour the oil into a large, heavy-based pan and heat until it forms a haze, then add the onion, ginger and green chillies. Sauté until softened, then add the *masala* and cook, stirring frequently, until the oil begins to separate out from it.

Add the water or stock and bring to the boil, then stir in the tamarind and cokums. Simmer for 5 minutes or so, then check the consistency. It should be like a pouring sauce, so if it is too thin, simmer for a little longer. Taste and adjust the seasoning if necessary.

Now put the fish in and simmer over a medium heat for 3–4 minutes without stirring. Remove from the heat, cover the pan and leave for at least 5 minutes to allow the fish to cook in the heat of the sauce. In this way it will have a perfect texture and will not break up.

VARIATIONS
This curry is also suitable for prawns, crab, lobster, mussels and even oysters. You can also use chicken (which will need sautéing separately first) or cauliflower and tomato with new potatoes. It is not suitable for red meats.

WHAT IS A *MASALA*?
A *masala* is a mixture of spices, seasonings and herbs, finely chopped or puréed together to form a savoury paste that is used as the basis for a dish. It can be a simple combination such as ginger, garlic and cumin or something much more complex. A fresh chutney, such as the green chutney on page 25, is also known as a *masala*.

A popular recipe that varies from region to region and even from home to home. The best fish to use pomfret, available from Chinese fishmongers or frozen from Indian shops. Either serve one fish per person as a main course or serve it as the Goans would, with a chicken curry, rice and Cachumber (see page 60) – in which case it will serve 8.

Fish Recheade

GOAN STUFFED FISH

Scale the fish, wash well and dry on kitchen paper. You now need to bone each fish. With a sharp, thin knife, make a cut the length of the backbone, then, on each side, use the knife to ease the fillet away from the bones, right down to the stomach cavity. Do not slit the stomach cavity open. All you are doing is separating the flesh from the bones but not completely filleting the fish. Snip either end of the backbone with scissors, then remove the backbone and the entire skeleton with it. Take out the guts as well if the fish has not been gutted. Remove any stray bones. Clean the abdominal cavity and wash the fish inside. Allow to drain well or pat dry with kitchen paper. Sprinkle the lime juice and some salt inside each fish and set aside.

For the stuffing, heat the oil in a pan, add the curry leaves and onions and sauté until golden brown. Add the masala and cook for a few minutes until you see the oil just oozing out through it. Stir in the shrimp powder and some salt, then add the chopped coriander. Remove from the heat and leave to cool. Check the seasoning and then apply the mixture inside the fish on either side. If possible, leave the fish in the refrigerator for a few hours before cooking. This will improve the flavour and the flesh will almost start to pickle, which greatly reduces the cooking time.

Heat some oil in a large frying pan set over a medium heat. Cook the fish until well browned underneath, then turn and cook the other side.

Alternatively cook the fish under the grill or on a barbecue. If grilling, brush the grill rack and the fish with oil. If barbecuing, place the fish on a piece of foil to prevent the skin coming off and brush the fish with oil before and during cooking.

4 x 500-g fish, such as pomfret, red snapper, grey mullet, mackerel, tilapia or sea bream

juice of 2 limes

oil for frying

salt

For the stuffing:

3 tbsp oil

15-20 curry leaves

4 onions, sliced

4 tbsp Piri-piri Masala
(see page 123)

4 tsp shrimp powder

4 tbsp chopped fresh coriander

salt

...lity, *tikka* is one of the best known of all Indian dishes. It is normally prepared with ...onkfish makes an interesting alternative. If monkfish is not available, select a chunky ...red snapper, pike or cod. To make chicken *tikka*, simply substitute chicken for the

Machli Kay Tikkay

MONKFISH TIKKA

400 g monkfish fillet, cut into 4-cm cubes (tikkas)

8 garlic cloves

5-cm piece of fresh ginger root

¾ tsp cumin seeds

¾ tsp coriander seeds

¾ tsp chilli powder

½ tsp ground turmeric

½ tsp garam masala (see page 123)

2 tbsp lime juice

50 ml mustard oil or groundnut oil

200 g Greek-style yoghurt

melted butter for basting

salt and white pepper

Rub salt and pepper into the monkfish and set aside. Put the garlic, ginger, spices, lime juice, oil and half the yoghurt into a blender and process to a smooth paste. When all the spices are well ground, transfer to a bowl and whisk in the remaining yoghurt. Taste and check the seasoning, adding more chilli if you wish. Mix in the fish cubes and check the seasoning again. Cover and leave in the fridge for at least 4 hours, preferably overnight.

Now cook the *tikka* either under a grill or on a barbecue, basting well with melted butter and turning the pieces until cooked through. (Put the tikka on skewers, if you like, to make turning easier.) If cooking under the grill, place the fish on the grill rack and make sure the heat is not too high. Alternatively, cook the fish in an oven preheated to 230°C/450°F/Gas Mark 8 for 8-10 minutes.

Dahi Maach

BENGALI FISH CURRY

500 g rohu (available in Bengali stores), river perch or pomfret, cut into large chunks

½ tsp ground turmeric

4 tbsp mustard oil or ghee

2-cm piece of fresh ginger root, crushed

5-6 garlic cloves, crushed

3 onions, very finely chopped

4-5 large dried red chillies, snipped into tiny pieces

250 g thick live yoghurt

3 bay leaves

2 green cardamom pods

1 tsp sugar

½ tsp garam masala (see page 123)

salt

Rub the fish with the turmeric and some salt and set aside for an hour or two. Drain well, reserving the juices, then rinse thoroughly and pat dry.

Heat the mustard oil or *ghee* in a large frying pan, add the fish and fry for about 2 minutes, just to seal. Do not allow it to colour. Remove the fish from the pan.

Mix the ginger, garlic, onions and chillies into the yoghurt and beat well. Transfer the mustard oil or *ghee* to a large saucepan and reheat. Add the yoghurt mixture and bring slowly to the boil. Add the bay leaves and cardamom and then the fish. Sprinkle in the sugar and *garam masala*. Pour in the reserved juices from the fish and bring to a simmer. Cover the pan, remove from the heat and leave for 5-7 minutes to allow the fish to cook through in the heat of the sauce. Check the seasoning, then serve with plain rice and mango pickle.

VERSATILE TURMERIC
You may wonder why I often toss fish and seafood in my recipes. There are several reasons but the most important are that it has antiseptic qualities, which help to kill bacteria; it is an excellent coagulant, so it prevents too much liquid seeping out; and finally it acts as a preservative.

Turmeric is so useful that in several remote areas of India it is carrried in trucks and cars on long journeys. This is not only for its medicinal properties but also to help mend burst radiators. If, for instance, a buffalo hits the car and the radiator is ruptured, a handful of ground turmeric put in the radiator collects against the hole and patches it up for long enough for you to get to the next town for repairs.

Chefs have been known to use turmeric to stop bleeding from cuts. A doctor at the Royal London Hospital was amazed when I applied it successfully to a cut in my arm. However, I don't recommend you try this at home!

Don't ask me why this is named Marie Kiteria. One day my chef, Mathias, suggested calling it this and the name has stuck. Marie Kiteria was his landlady in Goa and perhaps he had a secret affection for her – we shall never know.

You need to use mussels and clams on the half shell for this recipe. In Goa during the mango season, the half shells are left under a ripe mango tree. This attracts all the large red bully ants to the bottom of the tree so the pickers can scramble up and collect the fruit unhampered.

Shinanio Ani Tisreo Marie Kiteria

MUSSELS AND CLAMS IN COCONUT

Clean the mussels and clams and drain thoroughly. Toss in a bowl with the lime juice, turmeric and some salt, then set aside.

Heat 1 tablespoon of the oil in a large saucepan until hazy. Add the curry leaves, red chillies and cumin, then add the garlic and sauté for 1 minute. Add the onions and sauté until soft and pale. Stir in the coconut and cook for about 5 minutes, until it smells nutty and has turned pale golden.

Meanwhile, heat the remaining oil in a large heavy-based frying pan until smoking. Drain the mussels and clams, adding their juices to the coconut and onion mixture. Put the seafood in the frying pan and sauté briskly for 3–4 minutes, stirring or tossing occasionally. Do not overcook.

Add the seafood to the coconut mixture. Mix well, stir in the coriander and check the seasoning. Cook very briefly to blend the flavours, then serve immediately. It is best eaten with your fingers, although this can be a bit messy.

16 large mussels, on the half shell (preferably the New Zealand green-lipped variety)

32 large palourde (carpetshell) clams, on the half shell

juice of 1/2 lime

1/2 tsp ground turmeric

2 tbsp oil

12 curry leaves

2 dried red chillies, snipped into small pieces

1/2 tsp cumin seeds

6–8 garlic cloves, very finely chopped

2 onions, finely chopped

250 g fresh or thawed frozen grated coconut (see page 96)

2 tbsp chopped fresh coriander

salt

This dish is very common in Goa, although recipes differ. Always select small squid, as the tubes are more delicate and tender. Serve with a salad and perhaps some baked potatoes.

Bhorlelay Mankyo

STUFFED SQUID

4 tbsp Balchao de Camarao (see page 121)

16 baby squid, about 8–10 cm long, cleaned (tentacles retained and chopped)

150–200 g small raw prawns, chopped

3 hard-boiled eggs

1 tbsp chopped fresh coriander

2 tbsp oil

salt

Drain as much oil out of the *balchao* as possible (you need about a tablespoon). Heat the *balchao* oil in a frying pan over a high heat. Add the squid tentacles and the prawns and sauté until just cooked. Drain off the oil by squeezing the mixture against the sides of the pan until it is dry. Stir the prawn mixture into the *balchao*.

Separate the egg whites and yolks. Chop the whites finely and mash the yolks, then mix them both into the *balchao*. Stir in the coriander, check the seasoning and divide the mixture into 16 portions. Spoon the mixture into the squid tubes, then pinch the ends together and run a small wooden toothpick through in a zigzag fashion. Snap off the ends of the toothpick, so there is only about 1 cm jutting out at either side.

Heat the oil in a large, heavy-based frying pan, add the squid and cook over a high heat for about 2 minutes on each side. If small, the squid will cook very fast. Do not overcook or they will become rubbery. Serve immediately.

Illustrated on previous pages

Crab is found in abundance all round the coast of India. Stuffed crab is not especially an Indian dish but in Goa, where the Portuguese influence has led to many Western cooking techniques being adopted, it becomes very Indian with a hint of Europe. You could use crab meat instead of whole crabs and serve it in ramekins or gratin dishes.

Crab à la Goa

Remove the crab meat from the shells and set aside. Wash and dry the shells. Heat the oil in a large, heavy-based frying pan, add the ginger, garlic and green chillies and sauté for a minute or so. Add the onions and cook for 2–3 minutes, then add the *masala* and cook until the onions are soft and translucent. Add the ground coriander and turmeric and sauté, stirring, for 2–3 minutes. Stir in the tomatoes and cook for a few minutes longer, until the moisture has evaporated.

Now remove from the heat and season with salt. Mix in the crab meat, chopped coriander and peas, then check the seasoning. You might need to add a few dashes of lemon juice.

Stuff the crab shells with the mixture and cover with the cheese. Place under a hot grill to glaze, then serve with a salad.

VARIATION
Add chopped hard-boiled egg and a few chopped prawns.

SERVES 6

6 dressed crabs

2 tbsp sunflower or light olive oil

5-cm piece of fresh ginger root, finely chopped

5 garlic cloves, finely chopped

2 green chillies, finely chopped

2 onions, finely chopped

$1^{1}/_{2}$ tsp Piri-piri Masala (see page 123)

$1^{1}/_{2}$ tsp ground coriander

$^{1}/_{4}$ tsp ground turmeric

2–3 tomatoes, chopped

1 tbsp chopped fresh coriander

4 tbsp cooked peas

6 heaped tbsp grated medium-strong Cheddar cheese

lemon juice (optional)

salt

Lobster à l'Aguade

STUFFED LOBSTER

4 live lobsters, weighing
300-400 g each

1 tsp lemon juice

½ tsp ground turmeric

30 g butter

10 garlic cloves, finely chopped

2 green chillies, finely chopped

2 onions, finely chopped

1 tsp ground cumin

2 tsp ground coriander

4 slender spring onions, chopped

2 tbsp chopped fresh coriander

2 hard-boiled eggs, chopped
(optional)

2 tomatoes, deseeded and diced
(optional)

salt

Place the live lobsters in the freezer for about 2 hours, then prepare as follows: with a large, sharp knife, pierce each lobster just below the base of the head, then with a firm sawing motion cut down through the tail to split the lobster in half, leaving the shell joined at the bottom. Next turn the lobster around and split the head in half in the same way, again leaving the shell joined underneath. Break off the claws and set aside. Remove the meat, greenish liver and coral, if any, from the lobster shells and set aside; discard the stomach sac from just behind the eyes and the black intestinal vein. Wash the shells, put them in a large pan of boiling water, along with the claws, and weight down to prevent them curling. Remove the claws after 2 minutes (this brief blanching makes the meat easier to extract) but boil the shells until they are a good red colour. Rinse under cold running water, then drain well. The lobster shells are now your serving dishes.

Crack the claws and carefully remove the meat. Dice the raw lobster meat into 1-cm pieces and toss with the lemon juice and turmeric, then stir in the claw meat.

Heat the butter in a large pan until foaming but not browned. Add the garlic and chillies and sauté for 2 minutes. Then add the onions and cook until soft. Stir in the cumin and coriander and sauté for a minute or two. Raise the heat to high and add the lobster meat and spring onions. Mix the meat in briefly, then let it stay in the same position for a minute before you turn it around again. Do this only two or three times: the lobster will be cooked in 3-4 minutes, after which it will turn to rubber. Season with salt and remove from the heat. Remove the mixture from the pan with a slotted spoon and use to fill the shells. Place on serving plates and arrange the claws on the side as a garnish. Keep warm in a low oven.

Return the pan to the heat and boil to reduce the juices slightly. Add the coriander and the chopped hard-boiled eggs and diced tomatoes, if using. Pour the sauce over the lobsters and serve immediately, with Pulao (see page 102) or plain steamed rice.

I created this extremely popular dish in Goa and named it after one of our chefs, who unfortunately for him always ended up making it. You will need very large tiger prawns weighing about 80 g each. These are available frozen in blocks from Asian and Chinese shops and are usually labelled '6-8' (which refers to the number per pound).

Tiger Prawns Aureliano

8 large, unshelled raw tiger prawns

lime juice

50 ml oil

1-2 large green chillies, finely chopped

5 garlic cloves, finely chopped

½ green pepper, finely diced

1 onion, finely chopped

½ tsp cumin seeds, crushed

½ tsp ground coriander

1 tomato, deseeded and chopped

10-12 small prawns (cooked or raw), shelled and chopped

a pinch of saffron strands

the white of 1 hard-boiled egg

1 tbsp chopped fresh coriander

2-3 slices of bread, crusts removed, made into crumbs (or use a mixture of breadcrumbs and grated Parmesan cheese)

butter for dotting

salt and pepper

With a small, sharp knife, slit the prawns from head to tail, cutting almost all the way through the flesh but being careful not to separate the halves. Remove the black intestinal vein running down the back of each prawn, then skewer the prawn on a bamboo skewer (the type available from Chinese shops) and open it out like a butterfly. Sprinkle with lime juice and some salt and pepper, then set aside for 30 minutes.

Heat the oil in a frying pan and sauté the green chillies and garlic until softened. Add the green pepper and onion and cook gently until the onion is translucent. Add the cumin and coriander, stir for a minute and then add the tomato. If using raw prawns, put them in now and sauté for 1-2 minutes, until cooked through. Stir in the saffron. Remove from the heat and stir in the chopped egg white, fresh coriander and cooked prawns, if using. Check the seasoning.

Stuff the mixture into the opened prawns. Sprinkle with the breadcrumbs and dot with butter. Place the skewered prawns on a baking tray and bake in an oven preheated to 190°C/375°F/Gas Mark 5 for 10-12 minutes. Do not overcook. Place near the top of the oven so that they colour well. Alternatively, finish off under the grill, taking care not to burn the crumbs.

Serve with finely shredded salad and ciabatta or garlic bread.

TIP
For best results, gently warm saffron strands in a dry frying pan for a few minutes, then soak them in a little water before use.

This is a Parsee speciality and the cooking of the potatoes is quite typical, though methods vary. For instance, if my mother were to make this she would cook the prawns along with the potatoes. You can serve fried eggs on top of Masala Na Papeta, or bake beaten eggs on top of it.

Masala Na Papeta Ma Kolmi

PRAWNS WITH SPICY POTATOES

Wash the prawns and drain thoroughly. Sprinkle them with the lime juice and some salt and set aside.

Purée the ingredients for the *masala* in a blender, adding a little more vinegar if necessary to make a smooth, thick paste. Mix with the potatoes and marinate for at least an hour to allow the spices to penetrate.

Heat the oil in a large pan over a medium heat and sauté the curry leaves, garlic and green chillies for 2–3 minutes. Add the potatoes, along with all the *masala*. Sauté well for about 5 minutes, stirring frequently with a wooden spatula and scraping the base of the pan. Add just enough water to cover the potatoes, then cover the pan and simmer until the potatoes are almost done. Check whether the sauce around the potatoes is thick and rich looking. If it is too wet, simmer a little longer.

Raise the heat to high and add the prawns. Level out the prawns but do not stir or they will give off too much liquid and become rubbery. Cook on a high heat for 2–3 minutes, then season with salt to taste and sprinkle in the chopped coriander.

If the sauce is still too thin, transfer some of the liquid to a separate pan and simmer until reduced and thickened, then return it to the pan (this is a useful technique when cooking shellfish, which should never be overcooked). Serve with hot *chapatis* or crusty bread.

500 g shelled raw prawns

2 tsp lime juice

500 g potatoes, peeled and cut into 1-cm cubes

2 tbsp oil

5–8 curry leaves

8 very fresh green garlic cloves, with shoots, chopped (substitute 5 ordinary garlic cloves if necessary)

2 green chillies, finely chopped

3 tbsp chopped fresh coriander

salt

For the masala:

8–10 dried red chillies, cut up and soaked in $1\frac{1}{2}$ tbsp malt vinegar until softened

1 tsp cumin seeds

4–5 garlic cloves

$\frac{1}{2}$ tsp ground turmeric

1 small onion, chopped

Meat, Poultry and Game

This dry meat dish makes an ideal accompaniment to curries and rice. It can also be served simply with plain rice and yoghurt.

Ulathu

KERALAN DRY FRIED BEEF

Put all the ground spices in a dry frying pan and roast over a low heat, stirring, for 1-2 minutes. Leave to cool, then rub into the beef, with some salt. Cover and leave for at least 3 hours, or overnight in the refrigerator.

Heat half the *ghee* or oil in a frying pan, add the fresh coconut shavings and cook gently, stirring, until pale golden. Remove from the heat, drain on kitchen paper and set aside.

Heat the remaining oil or *ghee* in a separate pan and add any fat left from frying the coconut. Add the curry leaves and fry for 1 minute, then add the onion and garlic and fry until the onion is well browned. Remove from the pan with a slotted spoon and set aside. Add the beef and fry over a high heat for about 5 minutes, tossing well so that it browns on all sides. When the liquid begins to evaporate, reduce the heat and cook for a further 5-6 minutes. The meat should be about half done by now; if not, cover and cook for 5 minutes longer. Return the onion mixture to the pan and cook, uncovered, over a low heat until the meat is almost done. Add the coconut and continue cooking until the meat is tender.

2 tsp chilli powder

$3\frac{1}{2}$ tsp ground coriander

1 tsp ground turmeric

$1\frac{1}{2}$ tsp ground cumin

500 g rump steak, cut into 1-cm cubes

2 tbsp ghee or 3 tbsp oil

flesh of $\frac{1}{2}$ fresh coconut, cut into shavings on a mandoline or grater or with a swivel vegetable peeler

12-15 curry leaves

1 large onion, finely sliced

6-8 garlic cloves, finely chopped

salt

VARIATION
If you omit the coconut and substitute 3 tablespoons of Ginger/Garlic Paste (see page 61) for the garlic, this recipe becomes Parsee in style.

A simple recipe for making delicious lamb patties, or cutlets as we call them. A very old recipe was discovered in Bombay recently. However, this version is named after my mother-in-law, who makes similar ones using sheep's brains.

Freny Aunty Na Lacy Cutless

MINCED LAMB CUTLETS

1 onion, very finely chopped

oil for frying

500 g fresh lean minced lamb (frozen mince will make the cutlets watery)

5-cm piece of fresh ginger root, very finely chopped

6-8 garlic cloves, very finely chopped

2 green chillies, very finely chopped

1 tsp ground cumin

$1\frac{1}{2}$ tsp ground coriander

$\frac{1}{4}$ tsp ground turmeric

$\frac{1}{2}$ tsp chilli powder

2 tbsp chopped fresh coriander

2 tbsp chopped fresh mint

1 tsp lemon juice

3 slices of brown or white bread, soaked in a little water, then squeezed out into a ball

wholemeal flour

3-4 eggs

salt

Fry the onion in 1 tablespoon of oil until soft. Remove from the heat and leave to cool. Mix with all the ingredients except the flour and eggs and knead well. To check the seasoning, fry a small ball of the mixture and taste. Adjust the seasoning if necessary.

Shape the lamb mixture into small balls and flatten them to about 5 mm thick. Smooth the edges so that the sides are not frayed, using either the base of your palm or a palette knife. Spread some wholemeal flour out on a large flat plate or a tray and place each cutlet in it as you go along. Beat the eggs in a shallow bowl with some salt. Add 2 tablespoons of chilled water and beat until the egg white is totally absorbed.

Pour some oil into a large frying pan to a depth of 5 mm and set on the heat. Coat the patties with flour, then dip in the beaten egg and fry in the hot oil for about 2 minutes per side. They should be a nice golden colour with frilly edges. Drain on kitchen paper and keep warm in a low oven while you fry the rest. Serve with Tamota Ni Gravy (see page 20).

Use English, Welsh or Scottish lamb, if possible, as these are the most tender.

Dhaniawala Gosht

LAMB WITH CORIANDER

Roast the coriander and cumin seeds in a dry frying pan, then remove from the heat and crush lightly in a mortar. Roast the dried chillies and cinnamon in a frying pan over a low heat until they are aromatic and lightly coloured. Cool and crush in a mortar or a small grinder to the consistency of crushed peppercorns.

Heat the oil in a saucepan until almost at smoking point and add the lamb. Cook over a high heat until browned on all sides, then add the red chillies and cinnamon and sauté for a minute or two. Reduce the heat to medium, stir in the onions and cook, stirring constantly, until the base of the pan is scraped clean. Add a little water if necessary to help clean the pan. When the onions are translucent but not browned (they may go dark because of the pan juices, but this does not necessarily mean they are cooked), add the ginger, garlic and crushed cumin and coriander and sauté for a couple of minutes. Pour in water (or stock) just to cover the lamb. Season with salt, cover and simmer for 15-20 minutes. At this stage, if there is too much liquid, remove the lid and cook until the liquid has thickened and reduced. Stir in the tomatoes and cook on a medium heat until the lamb is tender and the gravy is thick, not watery. Mix in the fresh coriander and check the seasoning. Serve with plain steamed rice or bread.

2 tbsp coriander seeds

1 tbsp cumin seeds

4-5 dried red chillies, torn or snipped into pieces

2 x 2-cm pieces of cinnamon stick

4-5 tbsp oil

500 g boned leg of lamb, cut into 2-cm cubes

3 onions, chopped

1 heaped tbsp very finely chopped fresh ginger root

2 tbsp garlic, finely chopped

4 tomatoes, chopped, or 400-g can of chopped tomatoes

3-4 tbsp chopped fresh coriander

salt

Illustrated overleaf

Dhansak

SERVES 6 - 8

For the wet masala:

5-cm piece of cinnamon stick

6 cardamom pods

6-8 cloves

2 tsp cumin seeds

10 peppercorns

1 heaped tbsp coriander seeds

8-10 large dried red chillies

3 x 2-cm pieces of fresh ginger root, coarsely chopped

10-12 garlic cloves, coarsely chopped

30-50 g fresh coriander (stalks and leaves)

For the dry masala:

3-4 cardamom pods

3-4 cloves

2-3 star anise

1 heaped tsp cumin seeds

8-10 peppercorns

2-3 dried red chillies

2 tsp dried fenugreek leaves

One of the greatest and best-known Parsee dishes, Dhansak has often been grossly abused by restaurants in the UK. This recipe is the real thing. *Dhan* means rice and *sak* refers to the pulses (*daal*) and lamb that go with it. To a Parsee, Dhansak is always made with lamb. It is not complete unless accompanied by *cachumber*, or onion salad, and deep-fried lamb kebabs.

Cooking Dhansak is a lengthy, painstaking affair but not difficult. The end result is a great achievement and, if done well, will be acclaimed as a masterpiece. Start it a day in advance to serve for lunch the following day.

This recipe comprises five separate stages - the *daal*, the lamb, the *pulao*, the kebabs and the salad - each of which can be served as an independent dish as well. This typifies the depth and intricacy of authentic Indian cooking.

You need to make two *masalas*: the wet one is for cooking with the lamb, while the dry one is added at the end as a flavouring. Both can be prepared in larger quantities and stored in airtight jars for up to 6 months. Keep the wet *masala* in the fridge and the dry one in your larder. The dry *masala* is brilliant for flavouring meat dishes at the last minute.

DAAL

Wash the pulses and place them in a large heavy-based saucepan. Add enough water to cover by about 2 cm, then add all the remaining ingredients and bring to the boil. Reduce the heat and simmer, scraping the bottom of the pan frequently with a wooden spatula, until the pulses are tender. Purée everything until smooth, then cover and set aside.

LAMB

First prepare the *masalas*. For the wet *masala*, heat a large, heavy-based frying pan or wok, add all the ingredients except the fresh coriander and roast gently for about 5 minutes, stirring frequently. When the chillies and spices look roasted (i.e. they have changed colour slightly but are not actually discoloured) – remove and grind to a smooth paste in a blender, adding the fresh coriander and just enough water to process the mixture.

For the dry *masala*, roast the spices as for the wet *masala*, then grind to a powder in a spice grinder.

Now cook the lamb. Heat the oil in a large heavy-based saucepan, add the lamb and bones and sauté on a high heat until the meat is well coloured. Add the wet *masala* and cook until you see the oil separating out from it along the side of the pan. Add the water and some salt, cover tightly and cook on a medium heat for 20-25 minutes, stirring occasionally and adding a little more water if the mixture looks too dry.

When the lamb is cooked and you have a nice thick, rich gravy, stir the mixture into the puréed *daal*. Add half the dry *masala*, then taste. If it is to your liking, save the rest of the *masala* to serve with other lamb dishes. Or add the rest of the *masala* a little at a time, tasting as you go.

This is your *sak*. We Parsees call this *masala ni daar ma gos*, meaning lamb in lentils cooked in *masala*. You can serve it on its own with any kind of rice if you do not want to make the *pulao* below. However, your Dhansak will be incomplete.

For the daal:

100 g toover daal (yellow lentils)

50 g channa daal (yellow split peas)

50 g moong daal (mung beans)

100 g masoor daal (pink lentils)

1 small aubergine, diced

100 g pumpkin (peeled weight), diced

2 tbsp coarsely chopped fresh dill

1 colcasia leaf (arbi), if available

50 g fresh fenugreek leaves, or 1 tbsp dried leaves, toasted (see page 9)

6 tbsp prepared tamarind pulp (see page 28) or paste or 2 tbsp concentrate

100 g jaggery

2 tbsp chopped fresh coriander stalks

2 tbsp chopped fresh mint stalks

salt

For the lamb:

2-3 tbsp oil

500 g boned leg of lamb, cut into 2-cm cubes (ask your butcher to saw the bone up and give it to you)

150 ml water

chopped fresh coriander and mint, to garnish

salt

To make the remaining Dhansak *dishes (the* Pulao, Kebabs *and* Cachumber), *see overleaf*

Dhansak

continued from previous page

For the pulao:

5 tbsp oil

4 onions, finely sliced

1 tbsp chopped fresh mint

1 tbsp chopped fresh coriander

2-cm piece of cinnamon stick

3-4 cardamom pods

3-4 cloves

4-5 star anise

500 g basmati rice

about 2 tsp salt, to taste

For the cachumber:

1 large onion, finely sliced

10 fresh mint leaves, chopped

2 tsp chopped fresh coriander

1 green chilli, finely chopped

1 small tomato, deseeded and finely chopped

1 tsp malt vinegar

salt

PULAO

Heat the oil in a large pan, add half the onions and fry until crisp and light golden (see page 103). Drain well on kitchen paper and set aside with the mint and coriander (they will be used to garnish the rice just before serving). Add the spices to the casserole and cook over a fairly high heat for about 2 minutes, stirring, until dark and swollen. Add the remaining onions and cook gently, stirring frequently, until they are a deep brown colour. Add the rice and cook over a medium heat for 5-6 minutes, turning the rice regularly so that all the grains are evenly heated. Add the salt, then pour in enough hot water to cover the rice by about 2 cm. Stir for a minute, cover tightly and cook over a very low heat for 15-20 minutes. Check the rice from time to time, stirring from the bottom up with a wooden spatula. If it seems to be drying out, add more water, just a little at a time. When the rice is done, set aside but do not uncover the pan.

KEBABS

Follow the recipe for Freny Aunty Na Lacy Cutless on page 54, making the mixture into balls about 2-3 cm in diameter. Omit the flour and egg coating. Deep-fry the kebabs or, if you prefer, place them on a greased baking sheet and bake in an oven preheated to 200°C/400°F/Gas Mark 6 for about 20 minutes. You can also cook them under a grill if you rotate them regularly and check the cooking as you go along.

CACHUMBER

Mix all the ingredients together.

SERVING THE DHANSAK
Reheat the rice, lamb and kebabs if necessary. Garnish the *pulao* with the fried onions, mint and coriander, then dot the kebabs over the top. Garnish the *sak* with chopped fresh coriander and mint. Serve with the *cachumber*, and with fried *papads* (papadums) if you like. These should be lentil *papads*, not the Madras ones.

This is a typical simple Parsee lamb dish. It is one of my favourites, particularly when served with Dhan Daar Nay Vaghaar (see page 103).

Kharu Gos

LAMB WITH WHOLE SPICES AND ONIONS

Heat the oil in a heavy saucepan until a haze forms on top. Add the cinnamon, cardamom, cloves and red chillies. As soon as the spices swell and change colour, add the onions and sauté until well browned. Add the lamb and cook, turning occasionally, until browned on all sides. When the liquid in the pan has almost dried up, add the ground spices and the ginger/garlic paste and stir well. Then add some salt and enough water (or stock) to just about cover the lamb. Cover with a tight-fitting lid and simmer for 15-20 minutes, stirring from time to time and making sure the sides of the pan are kept clean.

Add the potatoes and mix them in well, then add the tomato, if using. Cover again and simmer until the lamb and potatoes are tender. Check the seasoning and sprinkle with some chopped fresh coriander. Stir some in as well, if you like, for an extra kick.

GINGER/GARLIC PASTE
Ginger/garlic paste forms the basis of most of India's cooking. In many recipes in this book I have listed finely chopped garlic and ginger separately to make life easier. However, in some recipes only a paste will do. Most supermarkets now sell separate jars of ginger paste and garlic paste. All you need to do is blend them together.

To make your own, take equal quantities of peeled garlic and ginger and work them to a paste with a mortar and pestle. Alternatively, purée them in a blender with a little water and some bland vegetable oil (not olive oil), stopping regularly to scrape down the sides. The paste will keep in the fridge for up to 2 months if you mix in a little oil to prevent spoiling.

2-3 tbsp oil

2-cm piece of cinnamon stick

3-4 green cardamom pods

1-2 black cardamom pods, if available

2-3 cloves

2-3 dried red chillies, torn or snipped into pieces

2 onions, chopped

500 g boned leg of lamb, cut into 2-cm cubes (ask your butcher to saw up the bone and give it to you)

1 tbsp ground cumin

1½ tbsp ground coriander

½ tsp ground turmeric

1½ heaped tbsp Ginger/Garlic Paste (see left)

1-2 large potatoes, peeled and cut into large chunks

1 tomato, chopped (optional)

chopped fresh coriander, to serve

salt

This spicy lamb dish is cooked with whole *garam masala*, fried red chillies, onions and yoghurt. It is similar to a classic *rogan josh* but hotter. If you have time, marinate the lamb with the ginger/garlic paste overnight.

Khadey Masaley Ka Gosht

LAMB WITH WHOLE SPICES, CHILLIES AND YOGHURT

SERVES 6

4-5 onions, finely sliced

200 g oil or ghee

8-10 large dried red chillies, broken or snipped into pieces

2-3 green chillies, slit lengthways

2 x 3-4 cm pieces of cinnamon stick

5-6 cardamom pods

4-5 cloves

4-5 peppercorns

1-2 blades of mace

500 g boned leg of lamb, cut into 2-cm cubes (ask your butcher to saw the bone up and give it to you)

2 tbsp Ginger/Garlic Paste (see page 61)

4-5 tomatoes, chopped, or 250 g canned tomatoes

200 g Greek-style yoghurt

1-2 tbsp chopped fresh coriander

salt

To garnish:

1 large potato, boiled, cut into cubes and fried until brown

2-3 eggs, hard-boiled and cut into wedges

Fry the onions in the oil or *ghee* until golden and crisp (see page 103) and then set aside. Fry the red and green chillies in the same oil for 2 minutes over a medium heat, until they are just getting darker, then set aside with the onions.

Reheat the oil or *ghee* in a large heavy-based saucepan until it forms a haze, then add the whole spices. Sauté for a minute or so until they swell and change colour. Add the lamb (and bone) and turn the heat to maximum. Stir once to level out the lamb, then cook, stirring as little as possible, until the lamb is well browned on all sides. (If you find the bottom of the pan is browning too rapidly, add a couple of tablespoons of water, scrape with a wooden spoon and continue cooking.)

Reduce the heat to medium. Add the ginger/garlic paste and sauté for 5-6 minutes. Cover the pan and cook for 20 minutes, stirring from time to time to prevent sticking. Do not worry, though, if the base of the pan is covered with a brown film. Add the tomatoes and some salt and continue cooking until the tomatoes have broken down.

Purée the fried onions and chillies with the yoghurt and add to the lamb. Cook uncovered for 5-10 minutes, then cover and simmer until the lamb is tender. Check the seasoning and stir in the coriander. If there is too much oil on top, skim it off and save for another lamb dish.

Remove from the heat and serve garnished with the fried potato and hard-boiled eggs. *Chapatis* or *parathas* make the best accompaniment.

This dish is regarded as a delicacy in some parts of Pakistan, where the best fenugreek (*methi*) grows. If you use fresh fenugreek for this recipe it will probably be the large variety. The small-leafed fenugreek is rarely available in the UK but if you do have it, reduce the quantity given below to 60 g and soak it in salted water for 30 minutes to soften the bitter flavour.

Methi Murgh

CHICKEN WITH FENUGREEK

500 g boneless chicken breasts

200 g Greek-style yoghurt

1 tsp lemon juice (optional)

50 ml ghee or oil

5-6 long green chillies, finely chopped (and deseeded, if you like)

8 garlic cloves, finely chopped

5-cm piece of fresh ginger root, half finely chopped, half cut into thin strips

300 g onions, finely chopped

1 tsp ground coriander

1 tsp chilli powder

200 g tomatoes, chopped

200 ml water

2 tbsp dried fenugreek (Qasuri methi), toasted (see page 9) or 120 g fresh fenugreek leaves, chopped

2 tbsp chopped fresh coriander

salt

For the whole masala:

5-6 green cardamom pods

1 black cardamom pod, if available

5-6 cloves

2-cm piece of cinnamon stick (in India and Pakistan acacia bark is used)

1 bay leaf

1 blade of mace

1 tsp cumin seeds

In India or at home, we would only cook chicken on the bone, but boneless breast makes the dish more special and easier to eat. Cut the chicken into whatever size pieces you prefer and remove the skin if you like. Beat the yoghurt with the lemon juice, if using, and some salt and mix in the chicken. Set aside for about an hour.

Heat the *ghee* or oil in a large pan until a haze appears on top. Reduce the heat and add the ingredients for the whole *masala* (putting the cumin seeds in last as they are more likely to burn). Cook until the spices are swollen and coloured, then stir in the green chillies, garlic and finely chopped ginger. When the garlic begins to turn golden, add the onions and the ground coriander and chilli powder mixed with about 4 tablespoons of water – this prevents the ground spices burning and also allows the colour to come through better. Cook until the onions are soft. Now stir in the tomatoes and cook gently until the fat begins to surface. Add the chicken and its marinade, then the water. Stir well and simmer, covered, stirring occasionally, for about 10 minutes, until the chicken is almost cooked. Stir in the fenugreek, coriander and the strips of ginger and cook for a few minutes more, until the chicken is done. Check the seasoning and remove from the heat. If you are using fresh fenugreek you will need to cook it a little longer.

Serve with soft corn tortillas, which are similar to Indian corn *chapatis*, or with warm Indian breads.

A delicate and mild dish that will please even the most chilli-fearing and unadventurous.

Malai Murg Tikka

CREAMY CHICKEN TIKKA

3 skinless boneless chicken breasts, cut into quarters

1 tsp lemon juice

1 tbsp double cream

3 tbsp Greek-style yoghurt

1½ tbsp finely grated Cheddar cheese

1 tbsp Ginger/Garlic Paste (see page 61)

6 cardamom pods, ground, or 1 tsp ready-ground cardamom

½ tsp ground cumin

½ tsp ground nutmeg

1 small green chilli, finely chopped (optional, but it gives a good flavour)

1 tbsp mustard oil

melted butter for basting

salt

Sprinkle the chicken with the lemon juice and some salt, place in a bowl and set aside.

In another bowl, whisk all the remaining ingredients except the melted butter together until the cheese blends in. Mix in the chicken, check the seasoning, then cover and place in the refrigerator for at least 3 hours, preferably overnight.

Like all other *tikkas*, this is best chargrilled. If you wish to cook it under a grill, place all the chicken pieces on a baking sheet, touching each other, baste with a little melted butter and cook under a medium-high heat until golden brown. Turn the chicken over carefully so that the pieces do not separate and grill until the other side is browned. The total cooking time should be about 12–15 minutes.

If chargrilling, don't place the chicken directly on the grill or it will stick. Instead, skewer the pieces and support the skewers so they are just above the grill. Cook, turning, until the chicken is browned all over.

This very popular Parsee dish is served on festive occasions such as weddings. The Parsee tradition of cooking with fruit, both fresh and dried, dates back to our Persian ancestry. You need to use Indian or Pakistani dried apricots, available from most Indian shops. They have a richer, less tart flavour than the ordinary variety. Stone them if you prefer, but we like to leave the stones in, then crack them later and eat the kernels.

This is very good served with crispy straw potatoes, or *sali*. *Chapatis*, bread or plain rice also make suitable accompaniments.

Jardaloo Ma Murghi

CHICKEN WITH APRICOTS

Soak the apricots overnight in about 250 ml cold water (or soak them for 2-3 hours in warm water), until swollen and soft.

Grind together all the ingredients for the *masala* and set aside.

Heat the oil in a large heavy-based pan and add the cinnamon sticks. After 1-2 minutes, when they are slightly swollen, add the onions and brown slowly. Then stir in the *masala* and sauté until the oil begins to separate from it. Add the chicken and sauté for about 5 minutes. Season, then add the tomatoes and apricots, plus any of the soaking water that has not been absorbed. Mix well, cover and simmer until the chicken is tender. If the sauce is too thin, uncover and cook for a few minutes longer until it has reduced and thickened. Stir in the chopped coriander and check the seasoning.

200 g dried apricots

4 tbsp oil

2 x 2-cm pieces of cinnamon stick

2 onions, chopped

500-600 g boned chicken, cut into 2-cm dice

4 tomatoes, chopped

1-2 tbsp chopped fresh coriander

salt

For the masala:

6-8 large dried red chillies

1½ tsp cumin seeds

1½ tbsp coriander seeds

2-cm piece of cinnamon stick

4-5 green cardamom pods

4-5 cloves

2 heaped tbsp Ginger/Garlic Paste (see page 61)

This is my version of a Goan recipe with obvious European roots. I love it and it has created waves on my menus in both England and Goa. Serve with garlic rice, made by sautéing some garlic and chopped spring onions in a little oil until softened, then stirring in cooked rice and heating it through.

Galinha Cafreal

CHICKEN GOAN-STYLE

8 chicken thighs

100 ml oil

2 medium onions, finely chopped

2-cm piece of fresh ginger root, shredded

1 large green chilli, shredded

¼ tsp ground turmeric

½ tsp ground cumin

½ tsp ground coriander

250 ml coconut milk (canned is fine)

For the masala:

5-6 large green chillies

5-6 black peppercorns

5-cm piece of fresh ginger root

8-10 garlic cloves

4-5 large deep-red dried chillies

4 tbsp chopped fresh coriander

2 tbsp lemon juice

1 tsp cumin seeds

2 tsp coriander seeds

salt

For the garnish:

oil for frying

1 large onion, cut into thick rings

1 large potato, peeled and finely sliced

1-2 tomatoes, sliced

First make the *masala*: grind all the ingredients except the salt to a thick paste in a blender or a mortar and pestle, adding a little water if you use a blender. Add salt to taste. Pierce the chicken thighs with a fork and rub the *masala* liberally into them. Cover and leave for at least 3 hours, preferably overnight in the refrigerator.

Heat the oil in a heavy-based frying pan set over a medium heat. Place the chicken in it skin-side down and allow to brown slowly, shaking the pan gently so that the skin does not stick. When golden, turn over and continue to cook until the chicken is done (test with a skewer; the juices should run clear). Transfer to a dish and keep warm in a low oven.

Put the pan back on the heat and add the onions, ginger, green chilli, turmeric, cumin and coriander. Sauté until the onions are browned, then stir in the coconut milk and simmer for 10-12 minutes, until the sauce has thickened to a pouring consistency.

Next prepare the garnish. In another pan, heat just enough oil to coat the base and then sauté the onion rings until brown. Remove from the pan and set aside. Add the potato slices to the pan and sauté until brown and tender.

Serve the chicken with the garnish. The sauce can either be served separately or poured over the chicken.

The term *vindaloo* comes from the Portuguese *vindalho*, meaning with vinegar and garlic. The Goans, of course, could not stop at this. With their spicy palate, they invented the *vindaloo* as we know it today. In the UK, *vindaloo* is much misunderstood, and is thought to mean a fiery hot curry. In fact a *vindaloo* is a hot, sweet and sour curry made with the notorious Goan red *masala*, and the degree of heat can vary from house to house, chef to chef. In Goa and Mangalore a *vindaloo* is always made with pork. However, it works well with several other meats.

This recipe is for a basic chicken *vindaloo*. You could substitute leg of pork, cut into 2-cm cubes, in which case reduce the quantity of oil by half and sauté the pork before adding the onions.

Vindaloo de Frango

CHICKEN VINDALOO

Heat the oil in a large saucepan, add the curry leaves and sauté for a few seconds. Add the onions and sauté until a deep golden brown. Stir in the *masala* and cook until the oil separates out from it. Add the chicken and cook until well browned. Stir in the stock or water, then add the tamarind and sugar, bring to the boil and simmer for about 15 minutes or until the chicken is cooked through. Season with salt and then serve with Pulao (see page 102) or crusty bread.

Peeled baby potatoes and cocktail onions or shallots may be added along with the chicken, or half way through the cooking time if you are using pork.

4 tbsp oil

a few curry leaves

3 onions, finely chopped

150-200 g Piri-piri Masala
(see page 123)

800 g chicken thighs

250 ml chicken stock or water

1 tbsp prepared tamarind pulp
(see page 28) or paste, or
1 tsp concentrate

1 tsp sugar

salt

Murghi Na Farcha

CURRIED CHICKEN FRIED IN EGG

2 tbsp oil

5-cm piece of cinnamon stick

4-5 green cardamom pods

3-4 cloves

1-2 green chillies, slit lengthways

8 chicken thighs

1 onion, finely sliced

2 tbsp Ginger/Garlic Paste (see page 61)

1 tbsp chilli powder

1 tsp ground cumin

2 tsp ground coriander

1/2 tsp ground turmeric

2 tomatoes, chopped

2 tbsp chopped fresh coriander

1 tbsp chopped fresh mint

oil for frying

3 eggs, beaten with 1 tbsp water

4-5 tbsp plain flour

salt

Heat the oil in a large frying pan over a medium heat. Add the cinnamon, cardamom, cloves and chillies and sauté for a minute, then push to one side of the pan. Add the chicken skin-side down, and cook until well browned, then brown the other side. Remove the chicken from the pan and set aside. Add the onion to the pan and sauté for 2 minutes, then stir in the ginger/garlic paste, ground spices, tomatoes and half the chopped coriander. Cook for a few minutes until you have a thick, dry mixture, then return the chicken to the pan (you could also add a couple of tablespoons of tomato ketchup; I must admit I do). Mix well, then cover and simmer for about 10 minutes, until the chicken is cooked through. Mix in the remaining coriander and the mint and leave to cool, covered.

Transfer the chicken to a plate, scraping off excess sauce, such as onion pieces. Do not wipe the chicken clean, however; it should have a light coating of sauce but should not be wet.

Pour some oil into a large frying pan to a depth of about 1 cm and heat until you see a slight haze. Coat the chicken pieces in the flour, then dip them in the egg, making sure they are completely coated. Lift them out of the egg, draining off excess, and then fry in the oil until golden brown. The egg must frizzle, giving a lacy texture. Do not discard the bits that float on the oil. When you serve the chicken you can sprinkle the bits of fried egg on top.

Drain the chicken on kitchen paper. Purée the sauce if you like, then reheat it. Dilute as necessary and serve with the chicken.

VARIATIONS
• Flavour the beaten eggs with spices, such as chilli powder, salt and a touch of turmeric.

• You could add tiny new potatoes, cooking them in the sauce. We Parsees love potatoes and no meal is complete without them.

Badak Chaanti Badami Pasanda

NUT-STUFFED DUCK BREAST

Mix together all the ingredients for the stuffing, then taste and adjust the seasoning if necessary. Chill until firm.

Trim some of the skin and fat from the duck breasts but do not remove it all. Slit the breasts horizontally through the centre, leaving them joined at one side. If you do this gently, using short strokes, the meat will separate fairly cleanly. Open out the breasts and lay them in a row. If necessary, beat them out a little to make them easier to roll up. Spoon the stuffing along the top edge of each breast (the wider end), then fold the edge over the stuffing and roll up into a sausage shape. Roll each breast in a piece of foil or greaseproof paper and place in a saucepan large enough to hold them all in a single layer. Pour in enough boiling water to come a little above the rolls, then cover and simmer for 20 minutes. Leave to cool in the liquid, then skim off any fat. Reserve the liquid.

To make the sauce, heat the butter in a large pan until foaming. When the foam subsides slightly, add the onions and sauté for 5–6 minutes, until translucent. Stir in the ginger/garlic paste and all the ground spices and sauté for 2–3 minutes. Next add the ground almonds and the cashew nuts and sauté for 4–5 minutes, stirring. Stir in 250 ml of the duck cooking liquid and simmer for 15 minutes, until fairly thick. If it gets too thick, add more cooking liquid or water. Leave to cool and purée in a blender. Return to the heat and bring slowly to the boil, stirring frequently.

Meanwhile, heat the *ghee* for the tempering in a separate pan and fry the whole spices and the bay leaves until dark and swollen. Add them to the sauce and stir well. Check the seasoning.

To serve, remove the foil or greaseproof paper from the duck breasts and place them in the sauce. Warm very gently so that the duck heats through. Place the breasts on a platter and pour the sauce over. Garnish with slivers of almond and pistachios.

SERVES 6

6 duck breasts

slivers of almonds and pistachio nuts, to garnish

For the stuffing:

150g ricotta or finely grated paneer

6–8 unskinned almonds, coarsely chopped

6–8 pistachio nuts, coarsely chopped

1 heaped tbsp sultanas

a generous pinch or two of ground cardamom

1 tbsp chopped fresh coriander

a small pinch of saffron strands

salt

For the sauce:

30 g butter

2 onions, sliced

1 tbsp Ginger/Garlic Paste (see page 61)

1/4 tsp ground turmeric

1/2 tsp ground cumin

3/4 tsp ground coriander

1/2 tsp chilli powder

100 g ground almonds

100 g cashew nuts

For the tempering:

1 tbsp ghee (or half butter/half oil)

2-cm piece of cinnamon stick

3–4 cardamom pods

3 cloves

2 peppercorns

1 blade of mace, broken in half

1–2 bay leaves

Toofan Mail was India's best-known mail train. thundering from Dehradun in the north to Bombay on the southwest coast. and boasting a very good dining car. Its name came to be used for any fast-moving vehicle or a product that sold fast.

I invented this *tikka* a few years ago and made it primarily with venison until ostrich. which has similar properties to venison. became available. I have included the recipe in this book partly because it has become such a popular dish in our restaurant but also because I know several people who have tried cooking ostrich at home and have not had very good results. This recipe should not disappoint.

Ostrich Tikka Toofan Mail

1 tsp salt

500 g ostrich (either fillet or leg), cut into 2-cm cubes, or into thin slices if barbecuing

2 tbsp sesame oil or mustard oil

2-cm piece of cinnamon stick

3-4 green cardamom pods

2-3 star anise

1 tsp fennel seeds

8-10 garlic cloves, coarsely chopped

2-cm piece of fresh ginger root, coarsely chopped

2-3 green chillies, coarsely chopped

3-4 large dried red chillies, torn or snipped into pieces

stalks from 1 bunch of coriander (save the leaves for garnishes, chutneys etc.)

250 g Greek-style yoghurt

1 tbsp lemon juice

Rub the salt into the ostrich meat and set aside.

Meanwhile. heat the oil in a pan. add all the remaining ingredients except the yoghurt and lemon juice and cook gently. taking care not to let them colour. Stir frequently until the heat has penetrated right through and the dried chillies are gently roasting. Leave to cool and then grind to a smooth paste in a blender with the yoghurt and lemon juice. making sure all the spices are fully ground.

Rub the paste into the ostrich meat and check the salt. Place in a clean bowl. cover and leave at room temperature for about 2 hours. then transfer to the refrigerator for 8-10 hours. For a dense meat such as ostrich, an overnight marinade is essential.

To cook the meat. grill under a high heat or on a barbecue. turning after about 3-4 minutes. Once it is well coloured on both sides. check a piece for tenderness. Be careful not to overcook it. Serve with a salad and Pulao (see page 102). to which you have added green peas..

This is a Rajasthani-style preparation, generally made with wild boar, although hare, venison, buffalo and game birds such as pheasant and partridge are also very good. This recipe is a simple version which will work with most meats. It is a pungent dish but, believe me, you will relish every morsel. It keeps very well in the refrigerator. Don't worry if the finished dish looks slightly greasy. In the days before refrigeration, food was sealed with a little fat as a means of preserving it.

Jungli Laal Maas

HOT RAJASTHANI GAME

500 g game meat, cleaned and cut into cubes (or cut into pieces on the bone if using birds)

½ tsp ground turmeric

3-4 onions, finely sliced

3-4 tbsp ghee

2 tbsp oil

5-cm piece of cinnamon stick

3-4 green cardamom pods

3-4 cloves

2 blades of mace

1 large dried red chilli, broken in half

300 g Greek-style yoghurt

2 tomatoes, chopped

chopped fresh coriander, to serve

salt

For the masala:

5-cm piece of fresh ginger root, roughly chopped

10-12 garlic cloves

6-8 long dark-red dried chillies

1 heaped tsp cumin seeds

1 tbsp coriander seeds

Rub the meat with the turmeric and some salt and set aside.

Next make the *masala*: put all the ingredients in a blender with a little water and blend to a thick paste.

Fry the onions in the *ghee* until golden brown and crisp (see page 103), then set aside.

Heat the oil in a large heavy-based saucepan and add any *ghee* left over from frying the onions. Add the cinnamon, cardamom pods, cloves, mace and red chilli and sauté over a medium heat for 2 minutes, until the spices change colour and swell. Do not let the chilli burn, but don't worry if it gets a bit dark.

Now add the meat and fry until evenly browned. Do not stir it too much or the oil will cool down and the meat will give off its juices. Add the *masala* and sauté for 4-5 minutes, until the oil begins to separate out from it. Add enough water to come about 1 cm above the meat, then cover the pan and simmer until the meat is about three-quarters done.

Purée the fried onions with the yoghurt and stir into the meat. Add the tomatoes and stir well, scraping the sides of the pan. Cover and continue to cook until the meat is tender. Check the seasoning and sprinkle with chopped fresh coriander. Serve with hot *chapatis* or flour tortillas.

These dry kebabs can be made with other game, such as venison, bison or even ostrich. The recipe is quite time-consuming but you can simplify it by omitting the skewering and frying at the end.

Jungli Soover Ni Seek Boti

WILD BOAR KEBABS

Put the meat in a bowl with the ginger/garlic paste, ground spices and lemon juice and mix until coated. Cover and set aside for 2-3 hours to allow the spices to penetrate, then transfer to the refrigerator for 5-6 hours, preferably overnight.

Heat 2 tablespoons of oil almost to smoking point in a heavy-based saucepan. Add the meat (reserving any liquid) and stir for a few minutes until well browned; don't be alarmed by the residue at the bottom of the pan. Add 1-2 tablespoons of water and the marinade juices, scrape the bottom of the pan with a wooden spatula, check the salt, then cover tightly and cook over a fairly low heat. After about 20 minutes, remove the lid and cook until the liquid has just about dried out and the meat has a thick coating on it and is almost cooked through. Remove from the heat and stir in the green chilli, coriander, ginger and garlic. Leave to cool, then mix once again. Next skewer the meat on small bamboo skewers, putting about 4 pieces on each. You can snap off one end if they are too long.

Spread the flour out on a large flat plate. Beat the eggs with a pinch or two of salt in a dish large enough to hold the kebabs. Pour enough oil into a large frying pan to fill it to a depth of about 1 cm and set it over a medium heat. If the oil gets too hot the egg will brown instantly and the kebabs will not heat right through. (If this does happen, place the kebabs on kitchen paper in a moderate oven for a few minutes before serving.)

Roll the kebabs in the flour, dip them in the beaten egg and fry for 1-2 minutes per side. Don't worry if there is extra egg on the skewers; this will help make the kebabs frilly.

Serve with chutney, such as the Green Chutney on page 25 or a hot, ketchup-type sauce.

500 g wild boar, cut into 2-cm cubes

2 tbsp Ginger/Garlic Paste (see page 61)

½ tsp ground turmeric

2 tsp ground coriander

1 tsp ground cumin

1 tsp chilli powder

½ tsp garam masala (see page 123)

1 tbsp lemon juice

oil for frying

1 large green chilli, finely chopped

1 tbsp chopped fresh coriander

1-cm piece of fresh ginger root, very finely chopped

2 garlic cloves, very finely chopped

3-4 tbsp plain flour

2 eggs

salt

Illustrated overleaf

This recipe dates back centuries. You can use whatever combination of game you like, depending on what is available. The koftas are served in a rich sauce but you could also serve them with Green Coconut Chutney (see page 36) or a raita (see page 118).

Shikari Nargisi Kofta

INDIAN GAME SCOTCH EGG

200 g venison
200 g hare
200 g wild boar
5-cm piece of fresh ginger root
8 garlic cloves
2 green chillies
3-4 fresh coriander sprigs
8-10 fresh mint leaves
1½ tsp salt
1 tsp garam masala (see page 123)
4 eggs
For the sauce:
2 tbsp oil
3 onions, very finely chopped
5-cm piece of fresh ginger root, chopped
8 garlic cloves
3-4 large dried red chillies
1 tsp cumin seeds
1 tbsp coriander seeds
½ tsp fennel seeds
5-cm piece of cinnamon stick, broken up
½ tsp ground turmeric
10-12 cashew nuts
1 heaped tbsp ground almonds
250-300 g Greek-style yoghurt
salt

Mince together the meat, ginger, garlic, chillies, coriander, mint, salt and *garam masala*, preferably twice to get a fine mince. Check the seasoning (fry a small piece and taste it), then set the mixture aside.

Hard-boil the eggs for 7-8 minutes, then drain. Cool gently under slow running water, shell the eggs and cut them in half.

Divide the mince into 8 and work each piece with your hands until soft and supple. Flatten each portion of mince in your palm and place an egg half in the centre. Pull the mince around the egg to enclose it completely and then shape it into a *kofta*, or ball. You can make it egg-shaped if you like or keep it round. The *koftas* are now cooked in the sauce but if you prefer you can deep-fry them or bake them in a moderate oven.

To make the sauce, heat the oil in a pan over a medium heat, add the onions and sauté until a rich, dark brown, stirring frequently. Meanwhile put all the remaining ingredients in a blender and purée until smooth. When the onions are browned, add the puréed mixture and stir continuously for 2-3 minutes, until it begins to bubble. Reduce the heat, cover and cook for 15 minutes, stirring and scraping the base of the pan from time to time. If it becomes too thick, add some water or stock.

Check the seasoning and cook for a further 10-12 minutes, until a thin film of oil comes to the surface. Add the raw *koftas* and cook covered for 20 minutes on a slow simmer. If you are adding them cooked you only have to simmer them for a few minutes until heated.

Crocodile has firm, lean flesh that tastes rather like pork. It is eaten in the heart of India, where crocodiles are found, by the Bhil tribes. This recipe is my invention, however, combining a traditional sauce with an unusual meat. *Ambotik* means sour and hot, and is a Goan curry, normally prepared with fish such as shark, skate or sting ray. Some supermarkets now sell crocodile meat or you can buy it from specialist butchers.

Crocodile Ambotik

Rub the lemon juice and some salt into the crocodile fillet and set aside.

Grind together all the ingredients for the *masala*, adding enough vinegar to make a smooth, thick paste.

Heat 3 tablespoons of the oil in a pan, add the onion and fry until golden brown. Add the *masala* and fry for 8–10 minutes or until the oil begins to separate out from it. Add the chopped tomatoes and cook for 4–5 minutes, until they have broken down. Stir in the water and simmer for 8–10 minutes.

Heat the remaining oil in a heavy-based frying pan and sauté the crocodile slices on high until golden brown on each side. Add them to the sauce and simmer for just a few minutes, until tender. Do not overcook as the crocodile meat can become tough. Check the seasoning and serve with steamed rice.

$1\frac{1}{2}$ tbsp lemon juice

500 g crocodile tail fillet, cut into slices about 8 mm thick

5 tbsp oil

1 onion, finely sliced

3 tomatoes, chopped

200 ml water

salt

For the masala:

10 dried red Kashmiri chillies

$\frac{1}{2}$ tsp cumin seeds

$\frac{1}{2}$ tsp ground turmeric

6–8 peppercorns

3 cloves

3 cardamom pods

1-cm piece of cinnamon stick

4–5 garlic cloves

1-cm piece of fresh ginger root

2 tbsp prepared tamarind pulp (see page 28) or paste, or 2 tsp concentrate

palm vinegar (substitute cider vinegar if not available)

Vegetable Dishes and Accompaniments

Do piaza is a Mughal term which, strictly speaking, means something that is added to or cooked with a meat dish. For instance, lamb cooked with okra is *gosht do piaza bhindi*. However, hotels and restaurants in India have corrupted the term so that it now refers to a dish cooked with onion cubes, or with double the quantity of onions.

Paneer Do Piaza

PANEER WITH ONION, GREEN PEPPER AND TOMATO

Heat the oil in a large pan, add the cumin seeds and cook for a minute or two, then add the onion, garlic and ginger and sauté until softened. Stir in the chilli powder, ground coriander and turmeric and cook for 1-2 minutes. Stir in the green pepper and tomato and cook until the pepper is softened. Now add the *paneer* and sauté for a further 4-5 minutes. Stir in the chopped coriander, salt to taste and the *garam masala* if using. Garnish with tomato wedges and serve.

VARIATION
Okra, diced chicken, prawns and fish can all be substituted for the paneer.

TO PREPARE PANEER
Paneer is a whey cheese that is now available in Indian food shops and some large supermarkets but is also easy to make at home. For 200 g paneer, bring 2 litres whole milk to the boil, then stir in 8 tablespoons of live yoghurt and simmer until it curdles. Strain through a sieve lined with a large piece of muslin. Once drained, transfer to a tray, fold the ends of the muslin over the solids and put a weight on top. Leave until all the moisture has been squeezed out. Store the pressed cheese in the fridge.

Before paneer is added to a dish, it must be cut into cubes and deep-fried in oil until golden, then drained and put in a bowl of water. Squeeze out well before use. Once fried, it can be stored in its bowl of water in the fridge for 6 days.

3 tbsp oil

1 heaped tsp cumin seeds

1 onion, cut into 8 pieces

6-8 garlic cloves, finely chopped

2-cm piece of fresh ginger root, shredded

1 tsp chilli powder

2 tsp ground coriander

a pinch of ground turmeric

1 green pepper, cut into 8 pieces

1 large tomato (such as a beef tomato), cut into 8 pieces

250 g paneer, cut into cubes, deep-fried and soaked (see left)

2 tbsp chopped fresh coriander

1 tsp garam masala (see page 123) (optional)

tomato wedges, to garnish

salt

Bhurjee means minced or finely chopped and generally refers to foods such as eggs, *paneer* and chicken. This simple recipe makes a great quick meal. It goes best with a pea *pulao* or *chapatis* and a sweetish chutney.

Paneer Bhurjee

SPICY MINCED PANEER

2 tbsp oil

6 garlic cloves, finely chopped

1 tbsp finely chopped fresh ginger root

1-2 green chillies, chopped

1 heaped tsp crushed cumin seeds

2 small to medium onions, chopped

$\frac{1}{4}$ tsp ground turmeric

$\frac{1}{2}$ tsp chilli powder

2 tomatoes, deseeded and chopped

400 g paneer, mashed with a fork

$1\frac{1}{2}$ tbsp chopped fresh coriander

$\frac{1}{2}$ tsp chaat masala

salt

Heat the oil in a saucepan, add the garlic, ginger and green chilli and sauté over a medium heat until the garlic begins to colour. Add the cumin and sauté for a minute or two, then add the onions. Cook until the onions are soft, then stir in the turmeric and chilli powder. Increase the heat to high and add the tomatoes. Sauté for 2-3 minutes, until the tomato juices begin to dry up, being careful the mixture does not stick. Lower the heat to medium once again and gently stir in the *paneer*. Cook until well heated through. Add salt to taste, then stir in the fresh coriander. Remove from the heat, sprinkle with the *chaat masala* and serve.

These croquettes are stuffed with nuts and cheese and simmered in a spicy spinach sauce. You can also make smaller ones and serve them as a delightful snack with any cream-based dip you like.

Malai Kofta Palakwala

POTATO AND CHEESE CROQUETTES WITH SPINACH SAUCE

Boil and mash the potatoes, drying them out well (see page 24). Season with salt and pepper.

For the stuffing, grate the cheese, then mix with all the remaining ingredients and check the seasoning. Shape the mashed potato into balls the size of an egg, then stuff each one with about 2 tablespoons of the filling. The easiest way to do this is to flatten the ball in your palm, add the stuffing, then pull the mashed potato around it with your fingers. Smooth the ball so it is round or egg-shaped and roll it in cornflour.

Deep- or semi-deep-fry the koftas in hot oil for 2-3 minutes, until golden brown. Drain well and set aside.

To make the sauce, heat the oil in a pan, add the onions and sauté until softened but not browned. Stir in the ground spices and cook gently for 1-2 minutes. Add the ginger/garlic paste and cook until the garlic gives off its unique aroma. Add the puréed spinach and season with salt. Cook for a minute or two, ensuring that the spinach does not discolour. Now add the fried koftas to the sauce. Pour in the cream and heat through gently. Check the seasoning, adding some *garam masala* if you like, and serve.

You can also serve this by placing the hot *koftas* on a platter and pouring the sauce over them or to one side. Do not leave the *koftas* in the sauce if you are not eating them straight away. They will keep in the fridge for up to a week if well cooked and tightly covered.

450 g floury potatoes, such as King Edward, peeled and chopped

cornflour

oil for frying

salt and pepper

For the stuffing:

50 g paneer or mozzarella

1 heaped tbsp chopped fresh coriander

2 tsp sultanas

2 green chillies, chopped

2-3 tbsp chopped mixed nuts

For the sauce:

2-3 tbsp oil

2 onions, finely chopped

1 tsp ground cumin

1 tbsp ground coriander

a pinch of ground turmeric

1 tbsp chilli powder

1½ tbsp Ginger/Garlic Paste (see page 61)

250 g fresh spinach, blanched, drained well and puréed

25 ml single cream

2-3 pinches of garam masala (see page 123) (optional)

salt

Illustrated overleaf

This unusual dish originally came from Kashmir, although without the potatoes. With a *pulao*, it makes an ideal accompaniment to a rich meat dish such as Khadey Masaley Ka Gosht (see page 62).

Saeb Aur Aloo Ki Subzee

APPLE AND POTATO BHAJEE

2 tbsp oil

a pinch of fenugreek seeds (about 8-10 seeds)

$1/4$ tsp mustard seeds

$1/2$ tsp cumin seeds

1 tsp coriander seeds, roasted and lightly crushed (see page 14)

2 green chillies, chopped

4-5 spring onions, including the green part, thinly sliced

2 potatoes, boiled, peeled and cut into 2-cm cubes

3 cooking apples (not too sour), cored and cut into 2-cm cubes

1 large tomato, deseeded and diced

sugar and lemon juice, to taste (optional)

1 tbsp chopped fresh coriander

salt

Heat the oil in a wok or large frying pan until hazy. Add the fenugreek seeds and then after 10 seconds or so add the mustard seeds. When they stop crackling, add the cumin and crushed coriander seeds and sauté for about $1 1/2$ minutes. Add the green chillies and sauté for a minute. Add the spring onions and sauté for 2 minutes, then add the potatoes and apples and toss lightly until well mixed. Add the tomato and cook for 2-3 minutes, tossing occasionally.

As soon as the apples soften slightly, check the seasoning and, if required, add a little sprinkling of sugar and lemon juice and some salt. Sprinkle in the coriander, toss and remove from the heat. Serve immediately.

VARIATION
At the last minute, throw in about 100 g blanched French beans, cut into tiny pieces. They will add crunch to the dish as well as making it look even brighter.

Khumb Mutter

CREAMY MUSHROOM AND PEA CURRY

Purée all the ingredients for the *masala* to make a smooth, thick paste. Heat the oil in a heavy-based pan, add the cinnamon and sauté for a minute or two over a medium heat. Reduce the heat and stir in the *masala*. Increase the heat to medium again and cook, stirring slowly with a wooden spatula, for 5 minutes: take care as the mixture will splatter. Cover and reduce the heat to low. Cook, stirring and scraping the base of the pan every minute or so, until the oil begins to separate out at the edges.

Add enough water to give the consistency of a thick sauce and simmer for about 20 minutes, until the sauce tastes cooked rather than raw. Season with salt, then add the shallots and simmer for a couple of minutes. Add the mushrooms and simmer for 5-6 minutes, until tender, then stir in the peas and tomatoes.

Simmer for 3-4 minutes and then stir in the cream and fresh coriander. Check the seasoning and serve sprinkled with the pistachios.

VARIATIONS
• **The sauce is also suitable for cooking chicken, fish, potatoes and other vegetables.**

• **Add deep-fried paneer (see page 81) to make a rich, creamy Paneer Khurma.**

2 tbsp oil

5-cm piece of cinnamon stick

12 shallots, peeled but left whole

500 g small button mushrooms

200 g blanched fresh peas (or thawed frozen ones)

10-12 cherry tomatoes

3 tbsp single cream

1 tbsp chopped fresh coriander

1 tbsp chopped pistachio nuts

salt

For the masala:

1 large onion, coarsely chopped

6 garlic cloves

2-cm piece of fresh ginger root

20 blanched almonds or 3 tbsp ground almonds

3 tbsp broken cashew nuts

3 green cardamom pods

3-4 tbsp Greek-style yoghurt

$1/2$ tsp ground turmeric

1-2 dried red chillies

This is a basic *kadhi* and below are some suggestions for items you can add to it to make a wonderful meal. It is perfect served plain as well. Just enjoy it with rice.

Dahi Kadhi

YOGHURT CURRY

SERVES 6

500 g Greek-style yoghurt

2 tbsp oil

½ tsp mustard seeds

10-15 curry leaves

1 tsp cumin seeds

¼ tsp asafoetida

3 tbsp besan (chick pea flour), sifted

½ tsp ground turmeric

2-3 green chillies, slit lengthways and deseeded

150 ml water

1 tbsp sugar

1 tbsp chopped fresh coriander

salt

Put the yoghurt in a bowl and whisk until smooth, then set aside.

Heat the oil in a saucepan until it forms a haze and add the mustard seeds. When they stop crackling, add the curry leaves and the cumin. Stir for a minute, being careful not to let the cumin burn, then add the asafoetida. Pull the pan off the heat and slowly add the chick pea flour, stirring all the time. Return to a low heat and cook, stirring with a wooden spoon. At first the flour will become hard but eventually it will soften and release the oil. At this stage add the turmeric and green chillies and cook for a minute or two longer.

Remove from the heat, allow to cool for a few minutes, then add the whisked yoghurt and mix until you have a smooth paste. (If you add the yoghurt over the heat it is likely to become lumpy.) Stir in the water and return to a medium heat. Bring to the boil, then add the sugar and some salt. Taste to check the seasoning: it should be slightly sour but also slightly sweet and savoury.

Boil for a few minutes until thickened to the consistency of a cream soup. If too thick, dilute to the consistency desired. Add the coriander and remove from the heat.

VARIATIONS

• Stir some deep-fried okra pieces (see page 118) or fried aubergine into the curry just before serving.

• Add raw sliced okra or raw banana pieces after the curry has come to the boil.

• Add some small onion *bhajias* (see page 10) just before serving.

Aloo Gobi Ki Tahiri

POTATO AND CAULIFLOWER PULAO

Heat the oil in a large saucepan until it forms a haze, then add the mustard seeds. When they stop crackling, reduce the heat slightly and add the green chillies, curry leaves, cumin and lastly the asafoetida. As soon as the cumin changes colour, stir in the garlic and cook until it begins to turn golden. Add the sliced onions and cook until translucent. Add the turmeric, followed by the potato and cauliflower. Sauté for a minute or two, then pour in the water. Cover and simmer until the potato is half cooked.

Add the rice, sauté for a minute or two, then stir in the lemon juice and enough boiling water to cover the rice by about 2 cm. Cover the pan tightly and simmer very gently, stirring every 2 minutes or so from the bottom up. The rice will fluff up nicely and should be cooked in about 15-20 minutes but if you find that all the water has been absorbed and the rice is still not done, splash a little more water around the edge and in the centre, then cover and cook for a few minutes longer.

You can also cook the *pulao* in an oven preheated to 200°C/400°F/Gas Mark 6 once you have added the boiling water. After 20 minutes, remove from the oven, stir with a two-pronged fork and, if need be, put it back in the oven for a few minutes until the rice is tender.

When cooked, check the seasoning and stir in the coriander. Serve with yoghurt and a light meat or vegetable curry.

5 tbsp oil
¼ tsp mustard seeds
2 green chillies, slit lengthwise
8-10 curry leaves
1 tsp cumin seeds
¼ tsp asafoetida
6 garlic cloves, chopped
2 onions, finely sliced
¼ tsp ground turmeric
1 large potato, cut into 2-cm cubes
1 small cauliflower, divided into small florets
100 ml water
400 g basmati rice
1 tbsp lemon juice
1 tbsp chopped fresh coriander
salt

This dish varies from place to place but this is a standard recipe and one that I feel works very well indeed. It makes a lovely accompaniment or starter. The stuffing mixture can also be mixed into yoghurt and served as a *raita*.

Bhareli Bhindi

STUFFED OKRA

20-30 okra (choose long, slender ones)

½ tsp ground turmeric

oil for frying

salt

For the stuffing:

125 g fresh or frozen grated coconut (see page 96) or 75 g coconut powder

2 large green chillies, finely chopped

1-2 tbsp chopped fresh coriander

½ tsp coriander seeds, finely crushed but not powdered

½ teaspoon cumin seeds, finely crushed but not powdered

2 tsp chaat masala

Wash the okra and wipe them dry. This is important or they will become gooey when cooked. Slit them open lengthways and sprinkle the turmeric and some salt inside. Mix together all the ingredients for the stuffing and season lightly. Stuff the okra until they are swollen but do not let them tear.

Pour a thin covering of oil over the base of a heavy frying pan and sauté the okra, in batches, for about 5 minutes, turning them until golden brown all over. Serve sprinkled with any remaining stuffing and accompanied by thick yoghurt.

Thoran

QUICK FRIED BEANS WITH COCONUT

2 tbsp oil

1 tsp mustard seeds

½ onion, finely chopped

3-4 green chillies, finely chopped

2-3 tsp desiccated coconut

¼ tsp ground turmeric

6-8 curry leaves

450 g French beans, cut into small pieces

salt

Heat the oil in a frying pan until very hot and add the mustard seeds. When they stop crackling, add the onion and green chillies, reduce the heat and cook gently until softened. Stir in the coconut, turmeric, curry leaves and some salt. Then add the beans and 6-8 tablespoons of water. Cover the pan and simmer for a few minutes, then remove the lid and cook, stirring, over a low heat until the liquid has evaporated.

VARIATION
This can also be made with cooked *channa daal* (split yellow peas) or lentils, or coarsely chopped fresh spinach or green peas.

Narial Aur Dahi Kay Subz

MIXED VEGETABLES WITH COCONUT

1 onion, sliced

1 potato, peeled and cut into cubes

1 small aubergine, cut into cubes

6-8 okra, cut into 2-cm pieces

1 small green banana, cut into cubes

1 drumstick, stringed and cut into 5-cm lengths

1 small snakegourd or a 15-20-cm piece, peeled, deseeded and cut into cubes

½ tsp ground turmeric

3-4 dried red chillies

2-3 large green chillies, chopped

300 g fresh or frozen grated coconut (see page 96) or 200 g desiccated coconut

½ tsp cumin seeds

200 ml Greek-style yoghurt

salt

For the tempering:

2 tbsp coconut oil

½ tsp mustard seeds

15 curry leaves

Put all the vegetables in a large pan, add the turmeric, red chillies and some salt, then pour in enough water just to cover the vegetables. Simmer until they are half cooked.

Grind together the green chillies, coconut and cumin seeds in a blender. When the cumin is well ground, add the yoghurt and whirl briefly. Add this mixture to the vegetables and bring slowly back to the boil, stirring constantly. Cook until the vegetables are completely tender. (This is how they are enjoyed in India but you could keep them slightly crunchy if you prefer.)

For the tempering, heat the coconut oil in a frying pan until hazy, then add the mustard seeds and curry leaves. When the mustard seeds stop crackling, pour this mixture into the vegetables, stir well, then check the seasoning. Serve with plain steamed rice or with crumpets – these can be steamed briefly to heat them and are perfect for soaking up the juices.

TEMPERING (*BAGHAAR* OR *VAGHAAR*)

Tempering is the term used to describe a last-minute flavouring of whole spices quickly fried in oil and then poured on to a finished dish to give it a final touch of glory. It is particularly common in the vegetarian cooking of the Gujerat and southern India and is almost always added to *daals* (lentil preparations). Although tempering is done primarily to add flavour, medicinal considerations are important too, as is often the case in Indian cooking. So the tempering for lentil dishes traditionally consists of spices that are well-known anti-flatulents, such as asafoetida, cumin and mustard.

Tempering is a very simple way of enlivening basic ingredients. Thus, if you were to boil, peel and cut up some potatoes and then pour over them some very hot oil to which has been added mustard seeds, cumin seeds, asafoetida and curry leaves, you have just tempered the potato and can call it *aloo bhaji*.

This can be served as a side dish or on its own with corn tortillas. In the north of India, where corn grows in abundance, a great many breads are made from corn. Instead of tortillas we eat corn *papads*, better known in the UK as *papadums*.

Gobi Aur Makki Kay Daney

CAULIFLOWER COOKED WITH SWEETCORN

200 g fresh or thawed frozen sweetcorn

1 tsp cumin seeds

2 tsp coriander seeds

3 tbsp oil

1 onion, chopped

1 tbsp Ginger/Garlic Paste (see page 61)

2 green chillies, chopped

1 small cauliflower, divided into small florets

2 tomatoes, chopped

2-3 heaped tbsp Greek-style yoghurt

2 tbsp chopped fresh coriander

salt

If you are using fresh sweetcorn, cook it in boiling salted water until tender, then drain and set aside.

Lightly roast the cumin and coriander seeds in a small dry frying pan, then crush them in a mortar.

Heat the oil in a pan, add the onion and sauté lightly over a medium heat until just about to brown. Add the ginger/garlic paste and green chillies and sauté for 2 minutes, then stir in the crushed coriander and cumin and sauté for a minute or two longer. Add the sweetcorn and cook for a minute, then stir in the cauliflower florets and sauté for a further 4-5 minutes. Put in half a cup of water and some salt and simmer until the cauliflower is half cooked. Do not overcook. Add the tomatoes and cook for a minute or two.

When the cauliflower is just tender, beat the yoghurt with a fork or a small whisk until smooth and add to the mixture. Simmer uncovered for 4-5 minutes, until you have a rich, creamy-looking sauce. Check the seasoning, sprinkle in the fresh coriander and serve.

VARIATION
Garnish with shredded green or red chilli and ginger. If you have some browned onions set aside, these will also add a great touch. Coarsely chopped roasted unsalted peanuts may be mixed with the coriander for extra flavour.

Potatoes are a great favourite in India and are cooked in a variety of ways. This recipe is very simple and easy to follow.

Aloo Ki Subzee

SPICED POTATOES

Heat a layer of oil in a large, heavy-based pan until it forms a haze. Add the mustard seeds, cumin seeds, curry leaves, asafoetida and green chillies and cook until the mustard seeds stop crackling. Add the onions and sauté until softened but not coloured, then add the potatoes. Sauté until the potatoes are evenly coated in the oil and spices, then stir in the ground spices, some salt and enough water to just about half cover the potatoes. Cover the pan with a tight-fitting lid and simmer on a low heat, stirring from time to time so the potatoes cook evenly. When the potatoes are almost done, add the tomatoes. Cook uncovered until the potatoes are tender and the sauce has thickened. Check the seasoning, stir in the coriander and serve.

VARIATION
You could also mix in some green peas at the end for a colourful finish.

oil for frying

$\frac{1}{2}$ tsp mustard seeds

1 tsp cumin seeds

8-10 curry leaves

$\frac{1}{4}$ tsp asafoetida

2 long green chillies, cut into 2-3 pieces each

400 g onions, finely sliced

750 g potatoes, peeled and diced

$\frac{1}{2}$ tsp ground turmeric

$\frac{1}{2}$ tsp chilli powder

1 tsp ground coriander

$\frac{1}{2}$ tsp ground cumin

250 g tomatoes, chopped

1 tbsp chopped fresh coriander

salt

A recipe from the Saraswat Brahmins of the Konkan. You will need to find unripe green mangoes for this. However, some of the red-skinned South American mangoes are very firm and could be substituted for green ones, although the flavour will be slightly different. If you use fresh coconut, you may like to garnish the finished dish with a few shavings, frying them in the oil before adding the mustard seeds etc (see page 106).

Aambey Chi Udda Methi

GREEN MANGOES WITH FENUGREEK AND JAGGERY

250 g fresh or frozen grated coconut (see below) or 150 g coconut powder

4-6 large dried red chillies

$\frac{1}{2}$ tsp fenugreek seeds

$\frac{1}{2}$ tsp ground turmeric

2 tbsp oil

$\frac{1}{2}$ tsp mustard seeds

2 tsp urad daal (white split gram beans)

15 curry leaves

$\frac{1}{4}$ tsp asafoetida

2-4 green mangoes, depending on size, peeled, stoned and cut into thin slivers

40-50 g jaggery

1 tbsp chopped fresh coriander (optional)

salt

Grind the coconut with the red chillies, fenugreek seeds and turmeric, then set aside.

Heat the oil in a pan until very hot. Test the heat by throwing in a few mustard seeds: they should crackle. When the oil is hot enough, add the rest of the mustard seeds, the white split gram beans, curry leaves and asafoetida. Once the gram beans have turned golden brown and give off a lovely nutty aroma, stir in the ground coconut mixture and sauté for a couple of minutes. Add the mangoes and a cup of water and simmer for 10-15 minutes, until the mangoes are almost tender. Put in the jaggery and simmer for a few minutes until the mixture has thickened. Taste and add salt if necessary. Stir in the coriander, if using.

TO PREPARE FRESH COCONUT
Where recipes call for grated coconut, desiccated coconut will not do. Instead buy a packet of frozen grated coconut, sold in Indian food shops, or buy a whole coconut and grate your own. Wet the coconut thoroughly and then mark a line all around the circumference with your fingers. Hold the coconut in one hand (over a bowl to catch the liquid) and hit it along the line with the back of a cleaver to crack it open; keep turning the coconut to work all round it. Drain out the liquid, then cut the flesh away from the shell with a sharp knife and peel off the skin. Grate the flesh on the fine side of a grater (or use a special coconut grater). One coconut should yield about 250 g.

Foogath derives from the Portuguese *refogado*, a thick onion purée which forms the basis of many slow-cooked Portuguese dishes. This Goan recipe has strayed a long way from its European origins and is more like a stir-fry. French beans can be used instead of carrots.

Cabbage and Carrot Foogath

Heat the oil in a large heavy-based saucepan over a high heat until a haze forms, then add the mustard seeds. When they stop crackling, reduce the heat to medium and add the curry leaves, cumin and red chillies. Sauté for a minute, then stir in the onions. When the onions turn soft, add the garlic and sauté for a minute or two, then stir in the turmeric, followed by the cabbage. Sauté the cabbage for a minute or two, then add the coconut. Sauté for 4-5 minutes, then mix in the carrots and check the seasoning. Cook for 2 minutes only; the carrots should still be crunchy. Sprinkle in a few drops of lime juice and add the coriander. Cover the pan, remove from the heat and leave to stand for 4-5 minutes.

Serve as an accompaniment or simply with hot crusty rolls.

2 tbsp oil

$\frac{1}{4}$ tsp mustard seeds

10 curry leaves

$\frac{1}{2}$ tsp cumin seeds

2 dried red chillies, cut into 1-cm pieces

2 onions, thinly sliced

6-8 garlic cloves, chopped

$\frac{1}{4}$ tsp ground turmeric

250-300 g white cabbage, shredded

250 g fresh or frozen grated coconut (see opposite)

250 g carrots, cut into thin strips

lime juice, to taste

1 tbsp chopped fresh coriander

salt

There are several different ways of preparing this Parsee dish. However, this is a simplified version, which I particularly enjoy. It makes a great side dish. Some Parsees like to add a little tamarind.

Bhaji Nay Dana Ma Kolmi

SPINACH COOKED WITH GREEN PEAS AND PRAWNS

500 g shelled raw prawns

½ tsp ground turmeric

1 tbsp lemon juice

2-3 tbsp oil

6-8 garlic cloves, chopped

1 tsp cumin seeds, roasted and lightly crushed (see page 14)

2 onions, finely chopped

5-cm piece of fresh ginger root, chopped

2 green chillies, deseeded and chopped

250 g fresh spinach, finely shredded

3-4 heaped tbsp cooked green peas

1 tsp sugar (optional)

1-1½ tbsp chopped fresh coriander

salt

Wash the prawns and then drain thoroughly. Place them in a bowl and mix with the turmeric and lemon juice.

Heat the oil in a large pan. Add the garlic and crushed cumin seeds and sauté for a minute or two, stirring, until the garlic is pale golden. Add the onions, ginger and green chillies and sauté until the onions are pale brown. Add the spinach and raise the heat to high. Sauté for a minute or two, then add the peas and swirl for a minute until they are hot. Add the prawns and some salt. Mix in briefly but do not stir too much or the prawns will give off their juices.

After a couple of minutes, when the prawns are almost cooked, add the sugar if you like, and the chopped coriander. Check the seasoning and remove from the heat. Cover and leave for a few minutes so the prawns finish cooking in the heat of the pan.

Fansi Jeera Tamatarwala

FRENCH BEANS WITH CUMIN AND TOMATOES

Heat the oil in a large frying pan, add the garlic, onion and cumin and sauté for a minute or two over a medium heat. Add the chilli powder. When the onion turns opaque, increase the heat to high and add the beans. Cook for 2-3 minutes, tossing them occasionally, then sprinkle with salt and add the tomatoes. Toss for a minute or so, then check the seasoning, add the fresh coriander, if you like, and remove from the heat. It's important not to let the beans overcook; they should be slightly crunchy. If water seeps out of them, it means the heat was too low.

Sprinkle over some *chaat masala* or a little ground cumin before serving.

2 tbsp oil

3-4 garlic cloves, finely chopped

1 onion, finely chopped

1 tsp cumin seeds, roasted and lightly crushed (see page 14)

$^{1}/_{4}$ tsp chilli powder

250 g slender French beans, trimmed

2 tomatoes, deseeded and chopped

1 tbsp chopped fresh coriander (optional)

salt

chaat masala or ground cumin, to serve

Illustrated on page 109

Rice, Pulses
and Breads

These simple croquettes can be made from left-over boiled rice. In Goa they are rolled in semolina instead of breadcrumbs, which gives a lovely crunchy texture. Serve with Fresh Tomato Chutney (see page 119).

Fofos De Arroz

RICE AND CHEESE CROQUETTES

Mix the cheese with the coriander, green chillies and paprika or chilli powder.

Season the rice with a little salt and mash it a bit with the palms of your hands until it is soft enough to be shaped. Shape into 8 balls. Take each one in the palm of your hand, flatten it, place some of the cheese mixture in the centre and then pull the rice around it, making sure the filling is completely covered. Form into a cylinder shape and then roll in the flour. Dip the croquettes into the beaten egg and then into the breadcrumbs. At this stage, they can be kept, covered, in the refrigerator overnight if necessary.

To cook, heat enough oil in a frying pan to give a depth of about 2 cm. Add the croquettes and fry until golden brown all over. Drain on kitchen paper and serve.

4 tbsp grated Cheddar cheese

$1^{1}/_{2}$ tbsp chopped fresh coriander

2 green chillies, chopped

1 tsp paprika or chilli powder

250 g rice, boiled and cooled

3-4 tbsp flour

2 eggs, beaten

dried breadcrumbs for coating

oil for frying

salt

Pulao, pilav, palav and *pilaf* - however it is spelled it is basically the same dish: rice tempered with a little oil and flavourings, then part-boiled, part-steamed. However, there are several regional and domestic variations. The recipe I give here is very simple and, hopefully, foolproof. Don't worry if you do spoil your rice: you can make croquettes with it the next day (see Fofos de Arroz on page 101).

Pulao

500 g basmati or other good long grain rice
3 tbsp oil or ghee
5-cm piece of cinnamon stick
2-3 cardamom pods
2-3 cloves
1 tsp cumin seeds
salt

Wash the rice in cold water and drain. Heat the oil or *ghee* in a heavy-based saucepan about 25 cm in diameter. Add the whole spices and fry for a minute or two until they swell and change colour. Add the rice and sauté for 2-3 minutes, stirring so that all the grains get evenly heated.

At this stage you must have a kettle of hot water ready. Rice normally absorbs three times its volume of water, so for 500 g rice you will need about 1.5 litres of water. However, the level of absorption can vary depending on the brand, so I recommend that you add just 1 litre of water to begin with. Stir well, dislodging any grains of rice from the side of the pan, add some salt and bring to the boil. Reduce the heat, cover and cook gently for about 15 minutes, until the rice is tender but still slightly firm. Stir every minute or so at first. If the water is absorbed too rapidly, add a little more but be careful not to make the rice too wet. Once it is done, loosen the grains with a fork, then cover and set aside until needed.

You can finish the rice in the oven if you prefer. After it has been simmering for 7-8 minutes, transfer it to an oven preheated to 190°C/375°F/Gas Mark 5 and bake for about 15-20 minutes. You probably won't need to add any more water in this case. If the rice is mushy (and this happens to the best of us occasionally), you can return it to the oven to dry out.

TIP
Always crack cardamom pods open before frying; this gives a better flavour and also prevents them exploding in the heat of the pan.

This is perhaps my favourite dish when served with a masala-fried fish. Parsee in origin, it is simple to make, nutritious, wholesome and, above all, delicious. The *vaghaar*, or tempering, is the final touch to a simple masterpiece, and can be used for other types of lentils, chick peas etc.

Dhan Daar Nay Vaghaar

PURÉED LENTILS WITH RICE AND FRIED ONIONS

Add the turmeric to the lentils and their soaking water and bring to the boil. Add some salt, reduce the heat and simmer, removing any scum from the top, for 30 minutes or until very tender. Stir in the butter and then purée the lentils and their liquid to a smooth paste with the consistency of a thick pouring sauce.

For the *vaghaar*, put the butter and oil in a small pan and heat slowly. Add the cumin seeds and then, 30 seconds later, the chopped garlic. Cook gently, stirring, until the garlic is golden brown, adding the chilli half way through, if using. Add to the puréed *daal*.

For the rice, bring a pan of approximately 1.5–2 litres of water to the boil with the bay leaves, cardamom and some salt. Add the rice and stir, then simmer for 8–10 minutes, until the rice is cooked but still slightly firm. Drain well and keep warm.

Finally prepare the fried onions. Heat the oil in a pan over a medium-high heat and add the onions. Stir them gently but frequently until they begin to turn light brown. At this point you will notice that oil is oozing out again and the onions are actually frying. This is a crucial stage; if you neglect them they will burn. Reduce the heat to low and keep stirring, breaking up any lumps and making sure that the onions stay beneath the oil. Have a sieve placed over a bowl (not a plastic one) and a fork kept handy. As soon as you see the onions turning a darker shade of brown, drain them into the sieve and loosen them with the fork, separating all the strands. If you don't do this the onions will continue cooking in the sieve and turn black. They have a unique way of holding hot oil and can burn very quickly.

Before serving, reheat the rice if necessary, and heat the lentils very gently, stirring with a wooden spoon or spatula and scraping the bottom of the pan. Mix in the chopped coriander. Serve the lentils on the rice, topped with the fried onions.

1 tsp ground turmeric

200g toover daal (yellow lentils), washed well, then soaked in water to cover by 2 cm for 2–3 hours

15 g butter

1 tbsp chopped fresh coriander

salt

For the vaghaar:

15 g butter

1 tbsp oil

1 tsp cumin seeds

8–10 garlic cloves, coarsely chopped

1 green chilli, cut lengthways into quarters (optional)

For the rice:

2 bay leaves

2 green cardamom pods

salt

400 g basmati rice

For the fried onions:

4–5 tbsp oil

2 onions, finely sliced

Ragda is a Gujerati dish of dried white peas, served with *pattice* or *poorie* (see pages 24 and 25). It can also be eaten as a side dish with rice. Use *channa daal* (split yellow peas) if you prefer, as they are more readily available.

When you are boiling beans or lentils, skim off the scum on the top as often as necessary, unless you are using a pressure cooker.

Ragda

CURRIED WHITE PEAS

200 g watana (dried white peas), soaked overnight and then drained

a pinch of bicarbonate of soda

3-4 tbsp oil

1 tsp cumin seeds

1 tbsp chopped fresh ginger root

1 tbsp chopped garlic

2 green chillies, chopped

2 onions, chopped

¼ tsp ground turmeric

1 tsp chilli powder

2 tbsp chopped fresh coriander

salt

Put the white peas in a pan with the bicarbonate of soda and some salt. Add just enough water to cover and then simmer until soft, topping up with a little more water if necessary. Drain the peas and reserve the cooking liquid.

Heat the oil in a large pan, add the cumin and sauté for 1-2 minutes without letting it burn. Add the ginger, garlic and green chillies and sauté for a minute or so, or until the garlic changes colour slightly. Add the onions and cook until soft and translucent. Mix in the turmeric and chilli powder and sauté for a minute or so, then stir in the boiled peas. Heat through and check the seasoning. Add the cooking liquid and cook for a few minutes until the mixture has a mushy texture. Stir in the chopped coriander and serve.

In the Punjab and Pakistan this traditional dish is served on most festive occasions. It is also very good with fried *paneer* stirred in.

Choley Pindi

PUNJABI-STYLE CHICK PEAS

If using soaked dried chick peas, put them in a pan with enough fresh water to cover by about 2 cm and boil until tender. Drain and set aside.

Heat the oil in a heavy-based pan, add the cumin and sauté for a minute without letting it burn. Add the onion, then the garlic, ginger and green chillies, and cook until the onion is softened. Stir in the tomatoes, followed by the yoghurt. Add the chick peas and cook, stirring frequently, until the mixture is thoroughly heated through. Add the *masala*, if using, or squeeze in a few drops of lemon juice, then stir in the coriander. Season to taste with salt and serve with *bhaturas*, *poories* or *parathas*.

VARIATION
If you can find them, gently roast and powder 2 tablespoons of pomegranate seeds. Sprinkle over before serving.

200 g kabuli channa (chick peas), soaked overnight and then drained, or 400-g can of chick peas, drained

2–3 tbsp oil

2 tsp cumin seeds, crushed

1 onion, finely chopped

5–6 garlic cloves, finely chopped

2-cm piece of fresh ginger root, chopped

2–3 green chillies, slit lengthways

2 tomatoes, chopped

4 tbsp Greek-style yoghurt

1 tsp channa masala or chaat masala, if available, or a squeeze of lemon juice

2 tbsp chopped fresh coriander

salt

Illustrated on page 108

This is often eaten for breakfast with a crusty roll in parts of Maharashtra and Goa.

Watana Ussal

WHITE PEAS WITH COCONUT

250 g watana (dried white peas), or other chick peas if you prefer, soaked overnight and then drained

5 tbsp oil

3 onions, sliced

250 g fresh or frozen grated coconut (see page 96) or 150 g coconut powder

6-8 dried red chillies

2 tsp coriander seeds

1 tsp cumin seeds

½ tsp ground turmeric

6-8 cloves

6-8 black peppercorns

1 tbsp white poppy seeds

1 tsp mustard seeds

12-15 curry leaves

1-2 tbsp chopped fresh coriander (optional)

fried fresh coconut, to garnish (see right)

salt

Put the drained peas in a pan with enough water to cover them by about 2 cm and boil until tender. Drain and set aside.

Heat half the oil in a heavy-based pan, add the onions and cook gently until light brown. Add the coconut and continue to cook until the coconut is brown. The mixture will stick to the pan, so it is important to use a heavy pan and to keep stirring and scraping the bottom with a wooden spoon. Stir in the chillies, coriander and cumin seeds, turmeric, cloves, peppercorns and poppy seeds and sauté for a few minutes on a low heat. Leave to cool, then grind the mixture to a thick paste, adding just a little water if using a blender.

Heat the remaining oil in a separate pan until very hot – test it by adding a few mustard seeds: they should crackle. Once the oil is hot enough, add all the mustard seeds to the pan. When they stop crackling, add the curry leaves and then stir in the spice paste. Sauté for about 2 minutes, then stir in the chick peas and enough of their cooking liquid to give a porridgy consistency. Taste and adjust the seasoning. Stir in the fresh coriander, if using, and garnish with fried fresh coconut.

TO FRY FRESH COCONUT
Make shavings of the coconut flesh on a mandoline or grater or with a swivel vegetable peeler, then sauté them in about 1 tablespoon of oil, stirring, until golden.

There can be no definitive recipe for *chapatis*. It is only through experience that you learn to judge the consistency of the dough and to roll it out deftly. When you attempt to produce smooth, round chapatis and end up plotting the world in different shapes, remember that even chefs and people such as myself with 20 years' experience cannot roll them out as skilfully as our mothers or wives. In hotels and restaurants throughout India where you see chapatis on the menu there is always a specialist employed. However, if you follow this recipe you will end up with a tasty bread that makes a good accompaniment to all sorts of foods, even if it is not perfectly shaped. Good luck.

Chapatis

MAKES 10-12

250 g wholemeal flour or medium chapati flour

1 tsp salt

1 tbsp oil, warmed

melted ghee or oil, for frying

Illustrated on previous pages: Choley Pindi *(see page 105) and* Fansi Jeera Tamatarwala *(see page 99)*

Sift the flour and salt into a bowl and stir in the oil. Gradually stir in enough cold water to give a firm dough, then turn out and knead for about 5 minutes, until the dough is no longer sticky. Cover with a bowl or clingfilm and set aside for an hour or two.

Divide the dough into 10-12 balls. Place each one on a lightly floured surface and flatten slightly with the palm of your hand. Then roll out into a round no more than 3 mm thick.

Heat a *tawa* or flat griddle, pour in about a teaspoon of melted *ghee* or oil and swirl to coat (or use a pastry brush). Dust off any excess flour from the *chapati* and place it on the pan. After about 30 seconds, flip it over with a fish slice and brush the top with *ghee* or oil. Cook for another 30 seconds, then flip it over again and brush the other side with fat (this is the Parsee style. The Gujeratis and several other Indian communities do not add *ghee* or butter till the very end.) When the *chapati* is cooked through, fold it in half, place in a container lined with paper towel or muslin and cover with a lid.

A good *chapati* is one that is cooked through but not burnt. If the pan is too hot, the *chapati* will brown instantly. You will probably get some brown spots on it in any case, which is fine unless you are a young Gujerati bride demonstrating your cooking skills to your future in-laws.

Vegetables can be included in the dough for *rotis* and *parathas*, adding flavour and giving them a distinct character. An entire chapter could be written on Indian breads but here is one simple variation on the basic dough.

Mooli Aur Pyaz Ki Roti

WHITE RADISH AND ONION ROTI

Sift the flour and salt into a bowl, stir in the warm oil, then knead in all the remaining ingredients with your hands so they release some of their juices into the flour. Gradually add enough cold water to make a firm dough. Turn out and knead for about 5 minutes, so the dough is well flavoured with the vegetables. If they are particularly moist and the dough gets sticky, knead in a little more flour. Cover the dough with a bowl and set aside for about half an hour.

Slowly heat a *tawa* or flat griddle but don't let it get too hot or the *rotis* will brown before they are cooked through. Divide the dough into 8 balls. Dip the tips of your fingers in oil and press down firmly on each ball to flatten it. Sprinkle with a little flour (combined with the oil, this gives a nice crisp coating). On a lightly floured surface, roll out each ball into a round about 4 mm thick – any thinner and it will probably crack because of the vegetables. Dust off any excess flour from the surface. Brush the griddle with oil and slap the *roti* on to it. After about 30 seconds, when it is beginning to loosen from the base of the pan, flip it over with a fish slice and then sprinkle the top with a little oil. Cook for another 30 seconds or so, then flip it over again and sprinkle the other side with oil. When the roti is cooked through, place it in container lined with paper towel or muslin and cover with a lid.

MAKES 8

250 g wholewheat flour or medium chapati flour

1 tsp salt

1 tbsp oil, warmed, plus oil for frying

1 small white radish (mooli), peeled and finely grated

1 onion, very finely chopped

1 tbsp chopped fresh coriander

1 small green chilli, finely chopped

Dips, Raitas, Chutneys and Pickles

Bapaiji, meaning paternal grandmother, is what my kids call my mother. This superb mayonnaise is made in a blender with whole eggs and is quite foolproof. It has always worked for me and for all the chefs who have trained under me. My mother taught me how to make it when I was just 12 years old. In India we keep it in small jars in the refrigerator for months on end. Mayonnaise is used quite a lot in Indian cooking, for parties and festive occasions. There is an Indian version of Russian salad made with vegetables, pineapple and mayonnaise.

Bapaiji Todiwala's Home-made Mayonnaise

Put all the ingredients except the oil in a blender and process on medium speed for about a minute. Put the oil into a jug so it will be easy to pour. Start the machine again and pour in the oil through the hole in the lid in a slow trickle. After 50 ml or so of oil have gone in, you can add it a little more quickly. Stop after a minute to check that the mayonnaise is blending well. Make sure that the blender goblet is not heating up. If this happens, you will have to stop for a while and remove the lid to allow rapid cooling. Continue adding the oil until you see that the well in the middle of the mayonnaise has closed up. At this stage, stop the machine, remove the goblet and give it a shake until the air bubble trapped inside bursts. Start the machine again and pour in more oil; you will see that a small well has started to appear again. Add the oil slowly until the well disappears or the machine begins to whine. Stop and shake the goblet again. Keep doing this until the well no longer forms after shaking. Your mayonnaise is now ready. If you are satisfied with the consistency before this stage is reached you can stop earlier. However, the more oil the eggs absorb, the longer the mayonnaise will keep.

Taste and adjust the seasoning, adding more lime juice and salt if necessary. Whisk them in either by hand in a bowl or by giving the mayonnaise another quick whirl in the blender.

2 free-range eggs

2 tsp good-quality wholegrain mustard

¾ tsp salt

¾ tsp sugar

1½ tsp Worcestershire sauce

1½ tsp lime juice

¼ tsp freshly ground pepper

about 250 ml unflavoured oil, such as sunflower

TIP
Use cold eggs and, if possible, cool the oil a little bit in the refrigerator until it gets cloudy but not too thick.

Yoghurt Chutney Dip

Prepare one quantity of the Green Coconut Chutney on page 36. Mix with thick yoghurt until you are happy with the flavour. You may need to thin it with a few drops of lemon juice or water. Stir in 1 finely chopped deseeded green chilli, some finely diced deseeded cucumber, a pinch of sugar and some chopped fresh coriander to taste.

Yoghurt, Tamarind and Chilli Dip

Mix 100 g Greek-style yoghurt with 1-2 tablespoons tamarind paste and 1 deseeded and finely chopped green chilli. Stir in 1½ teaspoons chopped fresh coriander, 1 teaspoon finely chopped fresh dill and 1 very finely chopped garlic clove. Season with 1 teaspoon sugar and some chilli powder and salt to taste.

Serve this with all sorts of snacks. It goes particularly well with smoked meats.

Mango Chutney Dip

Place all the ingredients in a blender and purée until smooth. It keeps indefinitely in a jar in the refrigerator.

250 g jar of sweet mango chutney
5-6 garlic cloves
2-cm piece of fresh ginger root
2-3 green chillies

This is a simple version of a classic Maharashtrian-style chutney. You can use ready-roasted peanuts or, for a better flavour, roast your own by placing them in a low oven until the skin flakes off.

Hot and Spicy Garlic and Peanut Chutney

The best way to make this is to grind all the ingredients together in a mortar and pestle until you have a thick, fairly smooth paste. Alternatively grind them in a blender, adding the oil a little at a time and scraping down the sides of the blender with a spatula with each addition.

15-20 garlic cloves
200 g lightly roasted peanuts
6-8 large dried red chillies
oil
salt

Illustrated overleaf: a selection of dips, raitas, chutneys and pickles

Raita

A *raita*, or *raitha*, is made by adding spices and chopped vegetables or fruit to yoghurt. The usual spices are chilli powder, ground cumin, *chaat masala* and salt. You can make *raitas* with finely diced deseeded cucumber, onion, tomato, boiled potato, boiled rice - and even crisply fried Chinese egg noodles, though they must be added just before serving. Fruits such as apple, orange, plum and papaya are all suitable - use your imagination to come up with interesting combinations. It is essential to use good thick yoghurt for *raitas*, and don't forget to add plenty of chopped fresh coriander.

Serve *raitas* as a condiment with semi-dry Indian dishes. They also make excellent dips for *poories*, *chapatis* etc. and are very soothing for upset stomachs.

Deep-fried okra is very popular with the Parsee community. This delicious deep-fried okra raita is a bit time-consuming to prepare but very simple.

CRISPY OKRA RAITA

oil for frying
200 g okra, trimmed and finely sliced
100 g Greek-style yoghurt
chaat masala
chilli powder
chopped fresh coriander
salt

Pour enough oil into a wok to fill it to a depth of 2 cm. Place over a medium heat, being careful not to let it get too hot. To test the temperature, throw in a couple of slices of okra; if they brown in less than a minute, reduce the heat and wait for a minute or two. Fry the okra (in small batches so that you can control the browning) until it is deep brown but not burnt - this will take about 3-4 minutes. The okra will absorb a lot of oil and then release it. Drain thoroughly in a colander or sieve and leave to cool.

Mix the yoghurt with *chaat masala*, chilli, fresh coriander and salt to taste. Mix in the crispy okra at the very last minute before serving, sprinkling some over the top as a garnish, too.

Although this is a fresh chutney, the tempering acts as a mild preservative. It also adds flavour. The chutney will keep for up to 10 days in the refrigerator if well sealed.

Fresh Tomato Chutney

Put the tomatoes, chillies, garlic, *chaat masala* and coriander in a glass or metal bowl and mix well, adding salt to taste. For the tempering, heat the oil in a frying pan until a haze forms and then add the mustard seeds. When they stop crackling, add the curry leaves, then the cumin and lastly the asafoetida. Immediately stir this into the chutney. It should make a hissing sound.

4–5 tomatoes, skinned, deseeded and chopped

1–2 green chillies, very finely chopped

2–3 garlic cloves, very finely chopped

1 tsp chaat masala

1 tbsp chopped fresh coriander

salt

For the tempering:

3 tbsp oil

$\frac{1}{4}$ tsp mustard seeds

6–8 curry leaves, shredded

1 tsp cumin seeds

a pinch of asafoetida, if available

My sister-in-law often prepares this simple chilli pickle and it is always very popular. You can also make it with fresh red bullet chillies or try vegetables such as carrot, swede, turnip or beetroot.

Mami June Nu Marcha Nu Achaar

AUNTIE JUNE'S GREEN CHILLI PICKLE

500 g large green chillies

250 ml mustard oil

2 tbsp coarse mustard

2 tbsp salt

1 tsp ground turmeric

¼ tsp asafoetida

10-12 garlic cloves, peeled and cut lengthways into quarters

2 tbsp lemon juice

Wash the chillies and leave to dry, then remove the stalks and cut the chillies into 1-cm pieces. Heat the mustard oil to smoking point and then leave until warm.

Put the chillies into a large bowl and mix in the mustard, salt, turmeric, asafoetida and garlic. Add the warm oil and mix in well. Transfer to a large sterilized preserving jar, tie a piece of muslin over the top and leave for a day or two. Then seal the jar tightly and place it on a windowsill where it will catch at least a little sunlight. Leave it for a month, or for 2 weeks if there is plenty of sun.

As long as the level of the oil in the jar is well above the chillies, the pickle should last for a very long time. Wipe the sides with a tissue each time you remove some chillies.

This traditional Goan dish can be served as a starter or stored and used as a condiment with curry or rice dishes.

Balchao De Camarao

PICKLED PRAWNS GOAN STYLE

Wash the prawns, sprinkle with a little salt and set aside.

Pour a thin layer of oil over the base of a heavy pan (if you are going to keep the *balchao* as a pickle it is essential to have some extra oil to act as a preservative). Heat the oil, add the onions and sauté, stirring frequently, until a deep golden brown. Be careful not to burn them but let them get as dark as possible. Add the curry leaves and then the *masala* and continue cooking until the oil has separated out from the *masala*.

Heat a little oil in a heavy-based frying pan until very, very hot. Drain the prawns thoroughly and put them in the pan, standing well back in case they splatter. Level them out but do not stir immediately or the oil will cool down and the prawns will release their moisture, thereby boiling instead of sautéing. As soon as the prawns are cooked and any liquid has dried, stir them into the *masala* and onions and simmer for a couple of minutes. Check the seasoning and stir in the shrimp powder.

Leave to cool, then transfer to sterilized jars and place in the refrigerator, uncovered. When chilled, seal the jars. If you are using very small prawns, the pickle will not need refrigerating. Large ones, however, will contain some moisture which will contaminate the pickle if not refrigerated.

TO SERVE AS A STARTER
Either use prawn *balchao* on its own or add some other shellfish to it, such as mussels, clams etc. Heat a little oil from the balchao in a pan and, if using shellfish, sauté them over a high heat for a few minutes. Add some chopped tomatoes and then stir in *balchao* to taste. Cook until saucelike, then sprinkle with fresh coriander and check the seasoning. Serve on toasted ciabatta bread.

400 g shelled raw prawns

oil for frying

6 onions, finely chopped

15 curry leaves

2 tbsp Piri-piri Masala (see page 123)

2 tsp shrimp powder

salt

A simple venison pickle which can be eaten fresh or stored for later use. If you like a bit of punch, add some slit green chillies just before frying the cooked venison.

Haran Nu Achaar

VENISON PICKLE

500 g venison haunch, finely diced
1 tsp ground turmeric
10 cloves
2 tbsp lemon juice
15-20 garlic cloves, peeled and cut into quarters lengthways
200 ml oil
3 onions, finely sliced
200 g jaggery
1 tsp ground cumin
1 tbsp ground coriander
1 tbsp chilli powder
1-1½ tbsp salt, to taste

Place the venison in a casserole, cover with enough water to come about 5 mm above the meat and bring to the boil. Add the turmeric, cloves, lemon juice and garlic. Reduce the heat and simmer for 20 minutes.

Meanwhile, heat the oil in a heavy-based pan and deep-fry the onions (in 2 or 3 batches) until deep brown. Stir them regularly and do not let them sit at the bottom of the pan for long. As soon as the onions are light golden, start transferring them to a sieve set over a bowl. By the time you have removed them all, they will be brown and will continue to brown in the sieve. Loosen any clumps with a fork and allow to drain well.

When the venison has been cooking for 20 minutes, add the jaggery. Continue cooking until the excess liquid has evaporated and the meat is lightly coated, then remove from the heat.

Reheat the oil from frying the onions, adding any oil from the bowl below the drained onions. Add the cooked venison to the oil, then almost at once add the cumin, coriander and chilli. Cook for a minute or two and add the onions. Mix well and check the seasoning. Put into hot sterilized jars immediately and seal. Ideally the pickle should be left to stand for at least a week before eating. You can, however, eat it right away as a condiment.

TIP

To sterilize preserving jars, wash them in a dishwasher if you have one. Alternatively, wash them in hot water, then microwave on High for 3 minutes. If you do not have a microwave put the jars (with their lids open) in a large pan with just enough water to keep them stable. Simmer for 15-20 minutes.

Piri-piri Masala

This is the classic Goan red *masala* and is one of the most versatile spice pastes in Indian cooking. It is equally useful with seafood, white meat and pork but it is not often used with red meats. If you cannot get palm vinegar, use cider vinegar instead.

Put the chillies, ginger, garlic and spices in a bowl, pour over the vinegar to cover, then cover tightly and set aside for at least 3 hours, preferably overnight. Grind to a smooth paste. If using a blender you may need more vinegar. Add it a little at a time, taking care not to make the paste runny.

This paste will keep indefinitely in a sterilized jar in the refrigerator. Use a Kilner-type jar rather than one with a metal lid. After using some of the *masala*, pour a spoonful of oil over the top of the remainder to prevent it drying out. If it does begin to look dry, add a little vinegar from time to time to revive it. Ensure that you wipe the sides of the jar clean with a tissue each time the level drops.

200 g large dried red chillies, broken or snipped into pieces

50 g fresh ginger root, coarsely sliced

10 garlic cloves, coarsely sliced

1 tbsp coriander seeds

1 tsp cumin seeds

5-cm piece of cinnamon stick

5-6 peppercorns

about 200 ml palm vinegar

Garam Masala

Garam means hot and so *garam masala* is literally a hot spice mix. It is usually added to dishes at the last minute as a flavouring, rather than cooked at the beginning like a *masala* paste. Most chefs have their own recipe which they guard fiercely, but the most common spices are cinnamon, cardamom, cloves, peppercorns, cumin, nutmeg, mace, star anise and coriander. The whole spices are roasted slowly, then ground and stored in airtight jars for use as required. Here is a simple recipe for a *garam masala* to make at home.

Put all the ingredients in a heavy-based frying pan and roast slowly until they are crisp and dry (or roast them in a low oven), taking care that they do not burn. Grind them to a powder and store in an airtight jar in the fridge.

1 nutmeg, coarsely crushed

10-12 green cardamom pods

2-3 black cardamom pods

10-12 cloves

2 x 5-cm pieces of cinnamon stick

2 tbsp cumin seeds

3-4 blades of mace

2-3 star anise

6-8 black peppercorns

4-5 bay leaves, crushed

Desserts and Drinks

Banana Fritters

Peel the bananas, cut them in half lengthways and then cut each piece in half again across the middle. Melt the butter in a large frying pan over a medium heat. Add the bananas flat-side down and sauté for $1\frac{1}{2}$-2 minutes on each side, until pale golden. Don't let them become too soft. Remove the pan from the heat, place the bananas on individual serving plates and keep warm in a very low oven.

Return the pan to a medium-high heat. Add the sugar and stir to dissolve, then add the rum (resist temptation to overdo the rum or the sauce will get bitter or taste too sharp). Ignite the rum with a match or a lighter (standing well back) and allow it to burn for a few seconds. You may find that the sugar caramelizes into lumps. If that happens, remove the pan from the heat and cool slightly, then add a little cold water, stir to dissolve the sugar and return the pan to the heat.

Pour in the cream and shake the pan in a circular motion for a minute or so until the cream begins to boil. Stir gently with a wooden spatula until the sauce thickens a little. Spoon the sauce over the bananas and serve immediately.

4 large bananas
30 g butter
3 tbsp demerara sugar
2-3 tbsp dark rum
150 ml single cream

Rawo is served on festive occasions as a good omen. Although it is traditionally prepared by women, please note that this is a man's version – mine. It makes a quick, simple and very tasty dessert and you will never again think of semolina as dull. You can decorate it with a few rose petals, if you like. Most rose petals are edible and they are widely used in India as a garnish on sweets, but make sure you choose unsprayed roses and soak them in water for a few minutes first.

Doodh No Rawo

PARSEE SEMOLINA PUDDING

$1\frac{1}{2}$ tbsp ghee
(or $1\frac{1}{2}$ tsp butter and 2 tsp oil)

6 almonds, chopped

6 cashew nuts, chopped

1 tbsp sultanas

15 g butter

100 g fine semolina

$2\frac{1}{2}$ tbsp sugar, or to taste

300 ml full cream milk

$\frac{1}{4}$ tsp grated nutmeg

$\frac{1}{4}$ tsp ground cardamom

$\frac{1}{4}$ tsp vanilla extract

$\frac{1}{2}$ tsp rosewater

a pinch of saffron strands

Heat the *ghee* in a frying pan over a medium heat, add the nuts and sultanas and fry gently until the nuts are light golden. Tip them into a sieve placed over a medium saucepan. Drain well, then place on kitchen paper to blot up any remaining fat.

Add the butter to the drained fat in the pan and melt over a medium heat. As soon as the butter begins to foam, add the semolina. Reduce the heat slightly and roast the semolina, stirring constantly with a wooden spoon or spatula, for 7–8 minutes, until slightly coloured. Be careful that it does not burn. Add the sugar and continue roasting for 4 minutes. Pour in the cold milk all at once and stir a bit faster now to prevent lumps. Simmer, stirring gently, for about 6–8 minutes, until the semolina is cooked. Add a little more milk if the mixture becomes too thick. It should have the consistency of thick porridge when removed from the heat, and will thicken further on cooling.

Stir in the nutmeg, cardamom, vanilla and rosewater and cook for a minute or two, then taste and add more flavourings if necessary. You may also prefer to add more sugar; personally I don't like it very sweet.

Transfer to a serving bowl and sprinkle with the fried nuts and sultanas. Serve warm. Leftover *rawo* is great even the following day and is good eaten cold as well.

TIP
Shake the chopped nuts in a sieve before frying. This way any small particles will be prevented from entering the fat and turning black.

Shahi Tukra

FRIED BREAD IN SAFFRON MILK

Heat the butter and oil in a large frying pan, add the bread, a few pieces at a time, and fry until golden brown on both sides. Transfer to a plate lined with kitchen paper to absorb excess fat.

Pour the milk into a heavy-based saucepan and bring to boiling point. Reduce the heat and simmer for 15-20 minutes, until it begins to change colour. Stir regularly with a wooden spatula, scraping the bottom of the pan to prevent burning, and keep the sides of the pan clean with a pastry brush dipped in iced water as described on page 132. Add the sugar and continue cooking until the milk becomes light brown in colour and gives off a nutty aroma. When the milk is ready it will be reduced in volume by at least a quarter and should coat the back of the spatula like a thin custard.

Stir in the saffron and cardamom and simmer for a further 2 minutes. Now add the rosewater and check the taste, adding more sugar if you feel it needs it. Leave until warm.

Place the cold fried bread slices on a platter and pour over the warm milk. Decorate with the chopped nuts and leave for 5-10 minutes, then serve. It is at its best when the bread is slightly crisp and not fully soaked.

30 g butter

4 tbsp oil

4 slices of white bread, crusts removed, cut in half

500 ml full cream milk

2 tbsp sugar, or to taste

a generous pinch of saffron strands

$\frac{1}{2}$ tsp ground cardamom

1 tsp rosewater

2-3 almonds, chopped

12 pistachio nuts, chopped

Pronounced 'alay baylay'. this is a traditional Goan sweet and is thoroughly enjoyable served with vanilla ice cream. cream or custard.

Alle Belle

GOAN COCONUT PANCAKES

SERVES 6

100 g plain flour

1 tbsp caster sugar

a pinch of salt

1 egg

150 ml coconut milk

1 tbsp melted butter, plus extra for brushing

a few drops of vanilla extract

a good pinch of grated lemon zest

a little oil or butter for frying

For the stuffing:

10-12 tbsp fresh or thawed frozen grated coconut (see page 96)

1 tbsp sultanas

75 g palm molasses or jaggery, coarsely grated

$\frac{1}{4}$ tsp ground cardamom

$\frac{1}{4}$ tsp grated nutmeg

Sift the flour. sugar and salt into a bowl. make a well in the centre and add the egg. coconut milk and melted butter. Whisk to a smooth batter, then stir in the vanilla and lemon zest. It should have a thin pouring consistency.

Mix together all the ingredients for the stuffing.

Heat a little oil or butter in a 15-18-cm frying pan. Pour in enough batter to coat the base thinly, tilting the pan to spread it. Cook for 1 minute. until lightly browned underneath, then flip over and cook the other side. Turn out and make the remaining pancakes in the same way.

Divide the filling between the pancakes and roll up. Place on individual serving plates. brush with melted butter and heat through under the grill.

A sweet made by both Maharashtrians and Goans. It is very nutritious and is often given to nursing mothers. Recipes differ from region to region, so treat this one as a guide and use your imagination to come up with variations.

Sabu Daney Chey Aloney

SAGO WITH CARDAMOM AND COCONUT MILK

100 g sago

250 ml milk

100 ml coconut milk (canned is fine)

150 g granulated sugar, or to taste

a pinch of salt

5 green cardamom pods, crushed

1 tbsp ghee (or 1 tbsp oil and ½ tbsp butter)

2-3 tbsp sultanas

10-15 cashew nuts, chopped

a few drops of vanilla extract and/or a few saffron strands (optional)

Optional decoration:

chopped pistachios and almonds

freshly grated nutmeg

Wash the sago lightly, put it in a bowl and add enough water to cover by about 2 cm. Leave to soak for 15 minutes. Drain through a colander, place in a heavy-based saucepan and add the milk, coconut milk, sugar, salt and crushed cardamom. Bring gently to the boil and simmer, stirring frequently to prevent sticking, for 15-20 minutes or until all the milk has been absorbed and the sago is swollen and translucent.

Meanwhile, heat the *ghee* in a pan, add the sultanas and cashew nuts and fry until the nuts are golden brown. If there is any fat left in the pan, drain the nuts and sultanas through a small sieve. If all the fat has been absorbed, place them on kitchen paper to blot them dry.

Taste the sago and add more sugar if necessary. You could also add some vanilla extract and, better still, a few threads of saffron. Stir in the sultanas and cashew nuts.

Pour the mixture into individual lightly buttered moulds and leave for about 5 minutes, then turn out on to a platter while still warm. Decorate with chopped pistachios and almonds and/or grated nutmeg, if you like. Serve warm or cold.

This may sound a bit weird but in fact it tastes really good. However, if you are very calorie conscious it is best to steer clear, or feed it to your friends instead.

Eeda Paak

EGG FUDGE

Lightly beat the eggs, then put them in a heavy-based non-stick pan with the sugar, butter, 4 tablespoons of ground almonds, rosewater, vanilla, cardamom, nutmeg and cream. Stir over a low heat with a wooden spatula, then when everything is well blended raise the heat slightly. Stir constantly, right up from the bottom of the pan or the egg will tend to settle and form lumps. After about 20 minutes the mixture should be very thick and pulling away from the sides of the pan (if it is still not thick enough, stir in the extra tablespoon of ground almonds).

Transfer to a greased 18-cm square baking tin and level the top. Sprinkle with the nuts and press them down a bit. Leave until warm, then mark into 2-cm squares with a palette knife. When completely cool, cut right through the squares and remove from the tin. The fudge will keep covered in the refrigerator for a few weeks. For the best flavour, warm it slightly before serving.

6 large free-range eggs

200 g caster sugar

125 g butter

4-5 heaped tbsp ground almonds

2 tbsp rosewater

a few drops of vanilla extract

6 cardamom pods, ground, or $\frac{1}{4}$ tsp ready-ground cardamom

$\frac{3}{4}$ tsp grated nutmeg

2 tbsp thick cream

1-2 tbsp chopped mixed nuts

Parsee Pav Makhan Nu Pudding

RICH PARSEE-STYLE BREAD AND BUTTER PUDDING

SERVES 4-6

1 litre full cream milk

5 eggs

150-200 g granulated sugar, plus extra for sprinkling

1 tbsp rosewater

½ tsp vanilla extract

½ tsp ground cardamom

½ tsp grated nutmeg

plenty of butter

5-6 slices of white bread

1 tbsp sultanas

1½ tbsp chopped mixed dried fruit

12-15 almonds, chopped

1 tbsp charoli (if not available, substitute pistachios)

Bring the milk to boiling point in a heavy-based saucepan, then simmer gently for about half an hour, keeping the sides of the pan clean at all times. To do this, immediately after the milk has reduced to a simmer, dip a pastry brush into a jug of iced water and brush down the sides of the pan. Repeat this every few minutes but make sure the brush is not dripping wet or it will dilute the milk. This might seem very time-consuming but it does give the milk a better flavour. Scrape the bottom of the pan frequently with a wooden spatula. The milk should eventually turn a shade darker and give off a nutty/toffeeish aroma. When it is ready it will be reduced by at least a quarter and should coat the back of the spatula like a thin custard. Remove from the heat and leave until warm.

Beat the eggs and sugar together until light and foamy - start off with a small amount of sugar, then taste after the milk has been added to see if you prefer it sweeter. Gradually whisk in the warm milk, then whisk for a minute. Mix in the rosewater, vanilla extract, cardamom and nutmeg.

Generously butter a baking dish about 1.5 litres in capacity and then sprinkle it with sugar until well coated. Butter the bread slices on both sides (trimming the crusts off if you prefer) and arrange half of them in a single layer in the dish, trimming them to fit. Sprinkle the sultanas and mixed fruit on top, then cover with the remaining bread and pour in the egg mixture. Sprinkle with the almonds and *charoli* and place in an oven preheated to 200°C/400°F/Gas Mark 6. Bake for 10 minutes, then reduce the temperature to 180°C/350°F/Gas Mark 4 and bake for 15-20 minutes or until a knife inserted in the centre comes out clean. The pudding should be golden and crisp on top; if necessary place it under a low grill to brown. Serve warm or cold.

As a kid I used to love this poured over hot *chapatis*, and the habit never died. If you like golden or maple syrup, this is a delicious new twist. Pour it over toast and enjoy it for breakfast, or serve with ice cream.

Gor No Seero

JAGGERY SYRUP

500 g jaggery
200 ml water

Cut up the jaggery into small pieces or shavings. Place it in a bowl and pour the water over. Microwave on High for 5 minutes or until the jaggery is totally dissolved and the mixture is boiling. Cool slightly, then strain through a muslin-lined sieve. Bottle the syrup and store.

You can also make the syrup in a pan on the stove: heat slowly until the jaggery has dissolved into the water, then boil for 5-6 minutes and strain.

Some types of jaggery absorb less water than others and the syrup may become too thin. If this happens, simply add more jaggery and simmer in a pan set over a low heat until dissolved.

Like good honey, jaggery tends to crystallize in the jar. Just warm it up before use, either in the microwave or by standing the jar in hot water.

Lassi

Lassi is a beaten yoghurt drink. It is quite substantial and many Indians would drink a good *lassi* in summer and not eat afterwards, or simply have a light snack. It is essential to use good-quality, creamy yoghurt, such as Greek-style. In India buffalo milk yoghurt, which has a 12-14 per cent fat content, is normally used; remember that low-fat yoghurt will not achieve the same lipsmacking result.

MANGO LASSI

To make this popular *lassi*, take about 150 ml yoghurt, ¼ glass of canned mango pulp (or 1 fresh mango, peeled, stoned and chopped), 4 ice cubes and some sugar if necessary. Place everything in a blender and give it a good whirl. Pour out into a tall glass and enjoy.

Other fruit such as strawberries, raspberries or papaya can be used.

MASALA LASSI

Put 150-200 ml yoghurt in a blender with a 1-cm piece of fresh ginger root, ¼ teaspoon of cumin seeds, a small piece of mild green chilli, 2-3 curry leaves, a pinch each of salt and sugar and a few ice cubes. Process until smooth, then serve with a sprinkling of very finely chopped fresh mint and coriander. You could try puréeing the herbs with the *lassi* but you may find the flavour an acquired taste.

JEERA LASSI

Blend 150-200 ml yoghurt with ½ teaspoon of cumin seeds (preferably roasted - see page 14), some salt and a few ice cubes. Both this and the Masala Lassi are good for upset stomachs, acidity and general digestive discomfort.

SWEET LASSI

Just yoghurt and ice cubes blended with a little sugar.

Limbu Panis

FRESH LIME WATER

This is sold in almost every major street of every large city in India. Fresh lime water is as popular as *lassi* but lighter and more refreshing. It helps to replace lost fluids and to control dehydration and nausea brought about by the extreme heat.

To make a simple *limbu panis*, put 2 tablespoons of freshly squeezed lime juice in a glass with 2-3 teaspoons of sugar and a pinch of salt. Add a little water and mix well untill the sugar dissolves, then top up with chilled water. Use soda water for a fizzy drink, if you prefer.

Salt and ground cumin are sometimes added. In India *kala namak*, or black rock salt, is used in the summer months to help prevent dehydration.

Tarbooj Ka Pani

FRESH WATERMELON JUICE

Peel and deseed a large piece of watermelon, being sure to remove all the seeds. Whizz the flesh in a blender with a few ice cubes, then transfer to a bowl. Stir in raspberry cordial (or Ribena) to taste. Rock salt may be added too, if you like.

By the Stock Exchange in Bombay, frantic brokers guzzle down cup upon cup of spiced tea every day. Different flavours and sizes are prepared according to demand.

A simple recipe is given here which will not only perk you up on a cold, dreary morning but also clear that unwanted crackle in sore throats. It doesn't matter what sort of tea you use but a small-leaf variety is best; don't go for anything particularly exclusive. The milk should be full cream, such as breakfast milk; skimmed does not give the same result. In India we use rich, creamy buffalo milk.

Masala Cha

SPICED TEA

Put a mixture of half milk/half water in a saucepan (quantities will depend on how many cups you are making). For every 2-3 cups, add 4-6 cardamom pods and a 1-cm piece of fresh ginger root, flattened with a heavy knife handle or a steak bat. Bring to the boil, simmer for a minute and then add the tea leaves - a little less than you would if you were making tea in a pot. Simmer for 3-5 minutes. Remove from the heat, cover and leave to infuse for a few minutes, then strain into the cups.

VARIATIONS
• A pinch of ground ginger or crushed peppercorns can be added when the tea is left to infuse.

• One clove for every 3 cups is sometimes included.

• A few saffron strands, some ground pistachios and ground cardamom can be stirred in after the tea is strained.

• A bruised fresh lemongrass stalk and a couple of mint leaves can be added when the tea is left to infuse. A 6-cm single layer of lemongrass is sufficient to flavour 3 cups.

• A small stick of cinnamon will yield yet another unique flavour, much enjoyed by the Pakistani people.

Glossary

Amchur

This is powdered mango, made by peeling, sun-drying and grinding unripe mangoes. It is one of the ingredients of *chaat masala* and is also used to flavour salads and chick pea and bean dishes.

Asafoetida (*Hing*)

The sun-dried gum of the ferula (a type of giant fennel), this used to come in a hard lump but is now more widely sold as a powder. Asafoetida is an anti-flatulent so it is often added to bean dishes. It is also used for other purposes in Ayurvedic medicine.

Besan

Besan is a chick pea flour used to make *pakoras* and *bhajias* and as a thickening agent for dishes such as *kadhi* (see page 88). It is also used in various sweets and fudges.

Cardamom (*Elaichi*)

Known as the queen of spices, cardamom is extensively used throughout India in meat, poultry, game and vegetarian dishes as well as sweets and desserts.

The best cardamom comes from Kerala in southwest India. There are many varieties but the most popular is the green. The brown cardamom, which is also used in Indian cooking, has large pods with a fibrous skin somewhat like a mini coconut.

Carom seeds (*Ajwain*)

These small brown seeds look like tiny cumin. They are used to make poultices to numb the pain from toothache and in fact some medicinal mouthwashes taste strongly of carom.

Because of their powerful flavour it is best to use carom seeds sparingly in cooking. They are added to batters and used to flavour green vegetables and *pulaos*.

Channa daal

Channa daal is a type of split chick pea but is sometimes confused with yellow split peas, which come from the same family and have a very similar flavour. Very popular in Punjab and the northern states, it is also used in southern and central Indian cooking, particularly in Kerala, where it is made into a sweet for one of its best-known festivals, the *Onam*.

Charoli

Also known as *chironji* in Hindi, this is the tiny kernel of the fruit of the same name. It most resembles a small bean and has a peculiar flavour - sweetish and almost musky. Used primarily as a garnish, it is not readily available in the UK, although some Indian shops may stock it. It is not widely used in India but since the Gujeratis love it you are likely to find it in stores run by them.

Chilli

Hari mirch, laal mirch, mirsang and *marcha* are some of the names by which this venerable member of the capsicum family is known in India. It is perhaps the most widely used ingredient in Indian cooking today, and very few savoury dishes require no chilli at all.

The Portuguese are credited with introducing chillies to India, although I find this hard to believe. They may well have brought with them from South America some of the varieties that grow in Goa today but surely they couldn't have been responsible for the countless different types of chilli cultivated in India.

In the past chillies were reputed to have medicinal properties and they are indeed rich sources of vitamins A and C. Their heat comes from a volatile oil called capsaicin. Generally, the smaller chillies are more lethal than their larger,

plumper cousins (although this cannot always be relied upon). For this reason I tend to specify large chillies in my recipes.

I like to use fresh green chillies to add a last-minute zing to savoury dishes and chutneys, while dried red chillies are more useful as a spice. In Indian cooking they are cut up and fried to release their flavour before other spices are added, and may be ground to make a *masala*.

Coconut (*Narial*)

Selecting a good coconut is crucial to Indians. The choice is more limited in the UK but look for a heavy nut that makes a good deep sound when tapped with a ring on your finger or your keys. Try out the sound of different coconuts to help you decide. Then shake it close to your ear and listen for the telltale sloshing of liquid inside. If the coconut doesn't contain much liquid it will not be very good for cooking. The giant coconuts from the west coast of Goa are the best I have ever seen but unfortunately they are seldom available elsewhere.

Coconut oil (*Narial ka tel*)

Extracted from dried coconut, this is available in various forms. Select a refined version if you are not familiar with the taste of coconut in your food. Coconut oil is very strong and should always be used with discretion. It is popular in southern India and Goa for cooking but is, in fact, primarily used as a hair oil. It makes an excellent massage oil and is also used in religious ceremonies.

Cokum

Sometimes referred to in English as the butternut berry, this is the small, round, deep purple fruit of a large evergreen tree and has a tart flavour. It is very versatile and is used extensively in Gujerat, Maharashtra and Goa - less so in other parts of India. It is regarded as a very good tonic for stomach disorders and skin ailments. Primarily used these days for flavouring curries, it is also sold as a syrup for making into a delightful summer drink. Most Indian food shops should stock dried *cokums* but if you cannot find them, use a tart variety of plum instead.

Colcasia leaves (*Arbi, arvi na patra*)

Arbi is a root vegetable that is widely used throughout India but especially in the north. The large, heart-shaped leaves are also used in cooking - one of the best known dishes is *patra*, or *patrel* as Parsees call it, where the leaves are stuffed with lentils and steamed, then sliced and eaten fried or cold. One or two leaves can be added to *dhansak* for flavour, although they are not essential.

Coriander (*Dhania*)

Both coriander seeds and the fresh green leaves are essential ingredients in Indian cooking. The seeds are valued not only for their flavour but also for their medicinal properties. The quality of ready-ground coriander is very good nowadays but for the best flavour you still need to grind the seeds yourself. Always roast them gently first (see page 14), then grind them to the consistency you prefer. Crushed roasted cumin and coriander can be used together as a condiment, added to dishes in the final stages of cooking to give them a lift.

Fresh coriander is an extremely versatile herb, not only in Indian cooking but in Western dishes too. Try substituting it for spinach in eggs Florentine for a delicious and unusual variation. It is also excellent with kidneys, liver and other forms of offal. Fresh coriander is widely available throughout the UK but if possible buy it from Indian shops, where it is usually cheaper than in supermarkets.

Cumin (*Jeera*)

This warm, sweetish yet slightly bitter spice has found its way into every corner of Indian cooking and it also has useful medicinal properties. The seeds are generally roasted to bring out their flavour (see page 14). To store cumin, keep it in an airtight jar, preferably in the refrigerator, where it will keep fresh for months.

Curry leaves (*Kadi patta*)

These small, oval leaves come from the *Murraya koenigii* plant, which eventually grows into a tree. They have a lovely powerful aroma and can be used fresh or dried, although dried ones do not have the same intense flavour.

If you can only find dried ones, you will need to use more of them. When you come across fresh curry leaves it is worth freezing them whole and using them direct from the freezer.

Drumstick (*Sekta ni singh, muska chey sango*)

This long, slender bean from an evergreen tree has a unique flavour, quite unlike anything else. Its stringy texture and very hard skin make it impossible to eat whole, so it is usually cut into sections and added to curries for flavour, then peeled before eating. You should be able to find it in Indian food stores.

Fenugreek (*Methi*)

Classed as a spinach in India, fenugreek is rich in iron, minerals and vitamins. It has small, oval, bitter-tasting leaves and is sold in India as a two-stage crop: the very tender young leaves resemble mustard cress in appearance and have a powerful flavour; the larger leaves are less strong and are cooked as a vegetable with meat and other greens.

Dried fenugreek is used extensively and could be said to act as the monosodium glutamate of northern Indian cooking. It is usually toasted first to mellow the flavour (see page 9).

Fenugreek seeds are used as a spice and are also very bitter, with a strong curry flavour. They are fried or roasted before use to reduce the pungency.

Garlic (*Lehsun, lasab, losun*)

Commonly believed in Indian folklore to be a destroyer of evil spirits, garlic is highly valued for its medicinal and culinary properties. It is an indispensable addition to most Indian dishes. In some parts of India, fresh green garlic is very popular and can be used to make excellent scrambled eggs.

Store garlic in a dry, airy place but do not leave it in the dark for too long or it will sprout, giving it a bitter flavour.

Ghee

Ghee is a form of clarified butter, traditionally prepared from homemade butter. In India, since buffalo milk is more commonly used than cow's milk and is very rich, a great deal of cream is collected in the house. Sometimes this is cooked slowly until only the fat remains, to make another form of *ghee*.

Ghee is available in two forms - pure *ghee*, made from butter, and vegetable *ghee*. Very pure *ghee* seldom solidifies.

Ginger (*Adrak, aadoo*)

This versatile root is added to just about everything from curries, spice blends, dressings and pickles to jams, sweets and drinks.

Ginger is an excellent tenderizer and is widely used as such in Indian cooking, particularly in tandoori marinades. Parsee households cannot do without ginger, sometimes even adding it to their tea (see page 137).

Green banana (*Kachcha kela*)

Green bananas and green plantains (which are larger and starchier than bananas) are used widely in Indian cooking, particularly by the Gujeratis, Maharashtrians, Goans and in southern India. However, the cooking methods vary greatly.

Green bananas and plantains are sold in Indian shops in the UK and you will also find a good choice in West Indian stores. They are often cooked in their skins to keep the flesh intact.

Jaggery (*Good*)

Jaggery is an unrefined sugar made in rural areas of India by boiling down sugar cane juice in large *kadhai*-type pans. It is used widely to make desserts and sweets and is also added to many savoury dishes. It is sold in blocks and has a delicious fudge-like flavour. You should be able to find it in most Indian food shops. If you cannot get it, demerara sugar is the best substitute, although the flavour cannot be compared.

Jaggery made from palm toddy is also available in the south of India, including Goa, and is much darker with a distinctly different flavour.

Kabuli channa

These are simply large white chick peas - the kind that are also popular in the Middle East and are readily available in the UK, either canned or dried. They are cultivated in the north of India, with the best-known chick pea dishes coming from the Punjab. In many parts of India they are known as *bengal gram*.

Khus-khus

Khus-khus, or white poppy seeds, are added to curries and kormas, both as a thickening agent and for their flavour. It is important to avoid stale seeds as they may taste rancid.

As a young child I spent some time in Madhya Pradesh/Rajasthan, where poppies were cultivated as a source of opium. The dried seeds were widely used in cooking and in those days we had to buy the entire bulb. The seeds rattled inside, making a *khus-khus* sound, which perhaps explains the name. I lived in a town called Neemuch, where a strong smell wafted in regularly from the world's largest opium refinery nearby. This ensured that you slept extremely well and never suffered from a stuffy nose.

Masoor daal

These small red or pink lentils are very versatile and easy to cook. They are used extensively in Indian cooking, from starters through to desserts.

Moong daal

These are mung beans. They can be cooked like any other beans but always remain slightly firm, so are seldom puréed. They are often used on religious occasions. A *moong kheer*, for example, may be served at a ceremony or at the beginning of a celebratory meal. They can be made into a delicious tasty snack known as *mogar* by first soaking them and then roasting in a wok or *kadhai* with a very little oil.

Mustard oil (*Sarsoon ka tel*)

This strongly flavoured oil has a pungent smell and is very viscous. It is popular in northern Indian cooking, particularly Bengal and the Punjab, whereas the south is dominated by coconut oil. Mustard oil is primarily used for making pickles. If you are using it in cooking it is best to heat it to smoking point, add a couple of red chillies and then remove from the heat. When cool, discard the chillies and use the oil as desired. This process mellows the pungent aroma and flavour.

Mustard oil is also used as a liniment and in several massage oils. As a hair tonic, it is thought to promote good, strong, lustrous, healthy hair.

Mustard seeds (*Rai dana, sarsoon, sansua*)

Though several varieties of mustard seeds are grown in India, the black ones are the most common. They have an excellent flavour when tempered. Mustard also has several medicinal applications and is widely used in the preparation of dishes for religious festivals.

Palm vinegar (*Taadi no sarco, boorachey vinaigir*)

Also known as toddy vinegar, this is the juice of the palm tree. The tree has a sort of a jugular vein which is tapped so that a milky fluid is released into pots tied beneath. The liquid is collected overnight and then drunk early in the morning.

After midday it begins to ferment vigorously and becomes undrinkable. It is then used for making bread and the remainder is stored in vats and matured into vinegar. A spirit is also distilled from the must and is known as *feni* in Goa and *arrak* in southern India. Toddy is warmed and served to invalids, particularly pneumonia patients. The taste is disgusting and it is little wonder that even though the British adopted the term 'hot toddy' they decided to give the patient whisky and hot water instead. Toddy vinegar is available in the UK in Filipino and other Oriental stores. It is not really suitable for Western-style cooking but is an essential ingredient in *piri-piri*, *balchao* and *patia*.

Paneer

Paneer is a simple fresh whey cheese. Its texture varies according to how it is made. For instance, Parsees make their *paneer* soft and creamy or set it in tiny cane baskets immersed in brine, like fresh mozzarella only softer and more delicate. The Punjabi-style *paneer* is the best known outside India. The whey cheese is pressed down with a heavy pot so that it becomes firm and hard. See page 81 for information on preparing this sort of *paneer* for cooking.

Rice

Chawal, chokha, dhan, xit (pronounced *zeet*), *tandul* - these are just some of the names by which rice is known in India. The Western world has come to think that there is only one rice in India - basmati. In fact there are hundreds of varieties and basmati is the least consumed. Such large quantities are exported that it has become too expensive for the average Indian to afford. It has always been a rice for special occasions because of its delicate flavour and aroma. However, several other varieties are equally treasured, some of which I find even more special - for example, *kolum*, or the silky one, from Gujerat, and *amba mohur*, meaning mango blossom. It is fortunate that most of these are virtually unknown outside India and so have preserved their unique qualities, free from hybrid strains or intensive cultivation.

Another myth about rice is that it is a staple food throughout India. It certainly is in the south, in regions such as Goa, Tamil Nadu, Kerala and Karnataka, and in most parts of Maharashtra, but in the northwest, where basmati is cultivated, wheat is the staple grain.

Most rice in India is aged before it is sold, and the older the rice the greater the value – just as with good wine. To judge rice, take a little in the palm of one hand and rub it with your other thumb to warm it. Then sniff it, as you would a good wine or spirit, rub again and sniff again. A good rice will give off a distinct aroma, which will give a connoisseur an indication of its age. An expert will also be able to tell this from the texture of the grain. With any rice it is worth checking that there are not too many broken grains and that it is not riddled with specks of white.

If you manage to buy really good rice from an Indian store (it will be packed in a gunny bag, a sack made from jute), remember that it will need washing and soaking thoroughly before cooking – unlike the well known prepackaged brands, which are heavily polished. Once opened, keep the remaining rice sealed in an airtight container.

If you are a rice enthusiast, then do try the wonderful range that is now available. We use red rice from the Camargue region of France and several organic Italian varieties daily in the restaurant and also like to try the oriental ones. All in all, rice is the grain of God to millions and should be revered accordingly.

Sev

Sev is chick pea vermicelli, available from most Indian food shops. A stiff dough is made from chick pea flour, then squeezed through a press into hot oil and fried until crisp. The *sev* is broken up and sold either on its own or mixed with other ingredients to make *chewda*, or *sev ganthia* – known as Bombay mix in the UK for some reason.

Shrimp powder (*Sukay suncta cho pito*)

Used as a flavouring in Goan dishes and Oriental curries, shrimp powder is also very popular in Burmese cooking. It is available in jars from Oriental stores, sometimes mixed with crushed dried chilli. If you buy dried shrimps or prawns, you can make your own shrimp powder by roasting them very slowly. When cold they turn crisp and can then be powdered in a small grinder.

Snakegourd (*Padwal*)

This a long, thin, gently curved green vegetable like a slender crooked marrow. In the north of India it is particularly enjoyed with pulses, while in the south it is used in mixed vegetable dishes such as *sambhar*. Snakegourd should be peeled, then split open, deseeded and cut into chunks before cooking. It cooks very rapidly.

Star anise (*Badian, fool patri*)

It is thought that the Chinese introduced this aniseed-flavoured spice to India. It is not very widely used in Indian cooking but many chefs add it to their *garam masala* and Parsees use it to flavour brown rice and occasionally in chutneys.

Tamarind (*Imli*)

This brown, bean-shaped pod of a tropical plant is a very important ingredient throughout India, imparting a unique tart flavour to food. Chutneys, curries, sauces, pulses, vegetables and rice dishes all benefit from the gentle touch of tamarind, added at the beginning of cooking or at the very end. It is also popular as a snack during school breaks. Tamarind vendors can often be seen outside schools selling fresh tamarind with a bag of salt and chilli powder as a dip. It is very sour eaten like this but children love it. Tamarind is also highly valued for its unique medicinal properties and is a particularly rich source of vitamin C. You will find it in Indian shops and some large supermarkets, sold as a compressed block, a concentrate or a paste. See page 28 for information on preparing tamarind.

Toover daal

These large yellow lentils are very common throughout India and are the most popular *daal* of all. There are a few varieties available and you may also see them with castor oil added to prevent them going rancid or succumbing to weevils.

Always store your lentils in an airtight jar and wash them thoroughly before cooking until the water turns clear. *Toover daal* is good on its own or mixed with other pulses.

Turmeric (*Haldi/Harad*)

This aromatic member of the ginger family is most readily available dried, either in its root form or ground to a powder, but it can also be bought fresh in some Asian food shops. The fresh root is a deep orange shade, only achieving its characteristic yellow colour when dried. Turmeric is a well known antiseptic and has several uses in Indian medicine (see page 42).

Urad daal

These are black gram beans, eaten either whole (very popular in northern India, especially the Punjab) or hulled and split to give a white bean (more popular in Madhya Pradesh and Rajasthan). When cooked, the split beans are unusually sticky and starchy. Do not overcook them or try to purée them or they will become glutinous, resembling a gruel rather than a *daal*.

Watana

These are dried white peas (actually a pale yellow colour) and are used throughout central and northern India. They need to be well soaked before cooking. If you are in a hurry, add a teaspoon of baking powder or bicarbonate of soda to the cooking water.

Index